THE
SOUL
COLLECTOR

LAURA DALEO

ALSO BY LAURA DALEO

Immortal Kiss
Bound by Blood
The Vampire Within
The Vow

AUTHOR LAURA DALEO

The Soul Collector is a work of fiction. Names, characters, places, and incidents either are the product of the author's imagination or are used fictitiously. Any resemblance to actual persons, living or dead, events, or locales is entirely coincidental.

Published in the United States by Author Laura Daleo, San Diego, California

Print ISBN: 9780997846188
ebook ISBN: 9780997846195

Cover Design: Laura Daleo / Ron Melanson
Editor: Dana Hook, RE&D

To my family, for their love and support.

Chapter 1

The biggest boxing match of the season landed on a Friday the 13th. But a little thing like superstition had no effect on the newcomer, Jonathan Bayfield, and heavyweight champion, Lou Turlock. The fight fans agreed, stomping their feet while chanting *"Fight! Fight! Fight!"* inside the packed, brightly lit arena. Sportscasters got up close and personal, claiming ringside seats for an in-your-face camera view.

Bayfield locked his gaze on his opponent, his right ear taking in Coach's words.

"Go to the body. Don't overreach. Straight punches. Got it?" Coach gripped Bayfield's shoulder. "Hey, eyes on me. Don't let him get inside your head."

Bayfield looked at Coach, giving him a slow nod, then reverted his focus back to Turlock, transmitting a defiant "this fight is mine" glare.

Turlock reciprocated, taunting Bayfield with a "we'll see" sneer.

The vein in Bayfield's forehead pulsed, spreading a surge of heat through his body. *A fist to the gut. That would show the arrogant prick he had something to worry about*, rattled through his mind. The ringside bell shattered Bayfield's thoughts, bouncing him to his feet. Turlock came out swinging, and Bayfield pivoted while throwing a right hook, catching the corner of Turlock's jaw. Turlock countered, landing a jab to Bayfield's chest. The blow forced the air from Bayfield's lungs, his body folding in half. But he quickly sprang upright, shaking off the sting, and fired off several consecutive punches straight into Turlock's gut.

Turlock wobbled back and the crowd roared, shouting, "Way to go, Bayfield!" Bayfield bounced back and forth on his feet, tapping his gloves to the crowd's cheers.

Turlock's own pulse battered against his eardrums. Where was the respect? He was a champion, and these morons had the nerve to cheer for a nobody, some kid who'd happened to land himself a good manager. Adrenaline tipped the scales on the fighter's rationality. Cognitive thought ceased. The whites of his eyes blazed as he hurtled his body like a weapon, slamming his skull against the kid's.

A crackling of bones ricocheted inside the ring, causing an eerie silence to fall over the area, before shouts from the crowd came from all sides. The ref barged in, spewing spit as he held Turlock back. Turlock's gaze traveled over the ref's shoulder, colliding with the kid's vacant stare. He knew that look; like no one was home. He'd seen it in his grandpa's eyes before he'd taken his last breath. An icy chill scurried down Turlock's spine as the kid crumpled to the mat. Turlock stood still as medics, judges, and more refs flooded the ring, surrounding the kid's lifeless body.

"I can't find a pulse."

"Start compressions."

Coach pushed his way through the chaos to Bayfield. "Jonathan, can you hear me?" Coach's voice shook. "Stay..." He blew out a breath. "Stay with me, buddy."

Bayfield's eyelids flew open, and with one push, he was on his feet. A weird and wonderful lightness affected his body, which made no sense, being as he weighed 200 pounds. Sounds rushed back, bouncing against his eardrums and forming words—Coach's words.

"Hold on, Jonathan. The ambulance is on its way."

Bayfield focused his attention on Coach. "Ambulance?"

"Just hold on."

Bayfield laughed. "What are you talking about? Coach, I'm standing right behind you. Turn around."

Coach made no attempt, his focus centered on something in front of him.

Bayfield's tone rose an octave. "Coach, what gives?"

No answer came, not from Coach, nor from any of the other people hovering around him. Bayfield skimmed the faces of the crowd, searching for a clue or hint to enlighten him on what the hell was happening. Why was everyone ignoring him?

"Step aside, people," security broadcasted with authority, herding the crowd back. "Let the paramedics through."

"Paramedics? Who got hurt?" Bayfield's gaze darted to Turlock, where men in dark blue suits surrounded him, escorting him toward the locker room. Bayfield let his gaze grow distant. He had no memory of the fight ending, and his boxing gloves were missing. No one acknowledged him. None of it made sense. He gave his head a good shake. "Gotta be an explanation for all this." As his vision cleared, it centered on the paramedics rolling a lifeless body away on a stretcher—*his* body!

His brain skidded to a stop—no pause, no rewind, no press play. Just a complete stop. Was he being punk'd? Was this some kind of sick joke? His gaze followed the stretcher, catching the tail end of it slipping inside the ambulance. Coach followed, his hands running through his salt and pepper hair. The look of sheer terror etched across Coach's pale face slammed against Bayfield's brain. This was no joke. This was real, and that ambulance was about to take off with his body.

Bayfield launched across the ring, catapulting over the ropes and sailing inside the ambulance seconds before the doors closed and the siren sang out. He plopped down next to Coach, his gaze transfixed on his own body lying across from him. One massive, purplish bruise swallowed up his bloodied forehead. Bayfield couldn't explain it—couldn't understand it. "I'm sitting here, but also lying there. How is that possible?" In a momentary shift, his eyes found Coach's, thirsty for an answer. None came. The silence sent a chill down Bayfield's spine.

A paramedic with tattoos blazing down his arms informed, "Got a pulse,"—his intense blue eyes narrowed—"but it's thready."

The paramedic behind the wheel, sprouting a six o'clock shadow, lobbed a reply over his shoulder. "Letting dispatch know we're five minutes out."

Coach gripped his hands, squeezing the blood from his knuckles. "Getting a pulse, even a weak one, is a good thing, right?"

The tattooed paramedic waited a good minute before saying, "For now, yes."

Chapter 2

The double glass doors of the emergency room entrance slid wide open, releasing an army of staffers in green scrubs. Dr. Clint Marcus, Chief Resident, surveyed the scene, his striking green eyes narrowing as he barked out, "What've we got?"

The paramedic with the tattoos rattled off, "Professional fight match gone wrong. Jonathan Bayfield, twenty-three years old. Blunt force trauma to the head, frontal impact, unresponsive, thready pulse. Intubated at the scene."

"Gone wrong how?"

"Got headbutted with his opponent's skull."

Dr. Marcus gave the paramedic a raised eyebrow before swinging the stretcher into center stage. "Where's the... Is the second ambulance on its way?"

The paramedic in need of a shave shrugged. "Not a mark on the other guy and standing on his own two feet when the cops hauled his ass away."

"Talk about a thick skull," Dr. Marcus mumbled.

The tattooed paramedic caught every word. "Doesn't it, though? Catch ya later for brewskies at McNally's?"

"Depends how the night goes." Thoughts of an ice-cold beer vanished as Dr. Marcus flashed a penlight into Bayfield's eyes. A militant glare gripped the corners of his eyes as he sounded off his demands. "I need a head CT, EEG, and get Neuro down here. We need a consult, stat!"

Bayfield backed away and sagged against the wall, his eyes never leaving his body.

Coach hovered by the stretcher and raised his voice over the chaos. "Is he going to be okay?"

"Who are you?" Dr. Marcus demanded, sizing up the broad-shouldered man standing in his way.

"I'm Coach—Coach Meyers. Jonathan's manager."

Dr. Marcus shooed him away. "Only family can be back here. You need to wait in the lobby."

"I'm also his legal guardian. I took him after his parents died ten years ago. Does that grant me rights? I have to stay with him. I'm all he's got."

Dr. Marcus laid a hand on Coach's shoulder. "Did you see what happened?"

Coach's face flushed red, grinding out his words through clenched teeth. "That bastard Turlock used his head as a weapon, slammed it into Jonathan's. Jonathan went down..." Coach's voice trailed off.

Dr. Marcus squeezed his shoulder. "He's here now, and in good hands. It might be a while before we have answers." He gestured toward the glass doors. "There's a waiting room just on the other side of those doors." Coach exhaled a deep breath and gave a hesitant nod, yet his feet made no effort to move. "I know it's hard to sit and wait. The instant I know anything, I'll come find you."

"Yeah, okay." Coach shuffled forward an inch, paused, and turned back to Bayfield, laying a hand on his shoulder. "Don't you think I'm leaving, 'cause I'm not. Just waiting around the corner." A pained look spread across Coach's face as he walked away.

Bayfield ran a hand over his buzz cut, feeling the coarse ends tickle his palm. Did he stay with his body or chase after Coach? Nothing good was coming out of those tests, that much he was certain, and what did it matter where he was when the news came? Not like anyone was talking to him. He stood unnoticed, a fly on the wall, and completely isolated. An icy chill slithered through his gut as the green scrubs vanished with his body. No matter how invisible he was, he couldn't do this alone, and sprinted after Coach.

Coach sat slumped in a chair, staring down at his hands. Bayfield knelt in front of him and whispered, "I'm scared. Really scared. Please, talk to me."

Coach made no effort to engage. Bayfield blew out an exaggerated breath, then sagged into a chair next to Coach. His vision caught sight of the people scattered about the room, bouncing a foot, glancing at the clock, or clutching their hands. He and Coach weren't the only ones awaiting news. Maybe he could get a reaction out of one of them—make them notice he was among them. He huffed and waved off the thought. Why bother? No one had acknowledged him so far, so why start now?

Awareness circled his brain, pushing him to his feet. What if he truly wasn't there? His eyes widened before darting about, searching for something, anything, that would collaborate his existence. The restroom sign caught his attention. Bayfield charged full force across the floor, skidding to a stop in front of the floor-length mirror inside the vacant restroom. A reflection stared back—his. He cupped a hand over his mouth, stifling a scream.

As the relief faded, he stepped closer, taking inventory. "Buzz cut, check. Dimples, check. Muscles, check." A splash of copper lit up his brown eyes. "That wasn't there before." He plastered a frown on his perfectly smooth, unmarked forehead. He stumbled into the wall. His fingers flew to his brow, inching across it. "How...? This can't be right." He blinked, shook his head, and looked again. No change. He jabbed a finger into his forehead and challenged his reflection. "I had a bloody bruise the size of Texas! No way does a thing like that just disappear. What the hell is happening to me?" He sank to the floor, shivering. Mental numbness gave his eyes a glazed look as he rocked back and forth, retreating from the world.

How long he cradled himself before picking himself off the floor, he had no idea, but when he entered the waiting room, he found Dr. Marcus seated next to Coach. Bayfield bolted, reaching Coach's side in four large strides.

Dr. Marcus's expression gave nothing away, and then he spoke. "Jonathan's skull is fractured. One of the blood vessels underneath was torn, causing blood to collect and put pressure on his brain."

Coach stiffened in his seat, and the magazine resting in his lap slid to the floor. "You..." His voice faded. He swallowed hard, then cleared his throat. "You can treat this, right?"

"I can't stay like this!" Bayfield blurted out. "He has to fix me!" Bayfield scrutinized both men, hoping for the slightest bit of recognition, and again, none came. He squeezed out an impatient snort. "Of course not. I'm invisible."

Dr. Marcus kept his tone relaxed. It worked better with emergencies. "Jonathan's on his way up to the OR with Dr. Yoo and his team."

"This Dr. Yoo, he's good?"

Dr. Marcus's lips spread into a rare smile. "One of the best."

Coach's shoulders drooped as he sighed. "Thank God. How long will he be in surgery? When can I see him?"

Bayfield groaned. "If you'd just turn around and open your eyes, I'm right—"

Dr. Marcus spoke over Bayfield, conveying the long laundry list of surgical tasks. "Dr. Yoo has to drain the bleeding in the skull cavity, then repair the torn vessel and fractured skull. If there's extensive swelling and damaged brain tissue, a portion may need to be removed, and a monitoring device will be placed in his skull to monitor pressure in the brain cavity. It's going to be awhile. As soon as we get a room setup for him, you can wait there."

An unfocused gaze claimed Coach's face. "That's a lot to take in."

"He's got a long road ahead of him. He's going to need your support."

Coach gave a firm nod. "And he's got it."

Bayfield couldn't get past the part about his brain being removed. Was that possible? Could they do that, just slice off a piece of brain? The skin on the back of his neck prickled, but not from Dr. Marcus's cheery speech. That eerie feeling of a pair of eyes burning into his flesh crept up behind him. The sensation pulled his gaze in its direction and landed on a young woman standing in the doorway, her brown eyes locked on him. Clad in cutoff shorts, a bikini top, and bare feet, she seemed as if she didn't belong. Her dark, soaking wet hair dripped beads of water onto the polished floor around her. Bayfield blinked, then did a double take as that same hint of copper flashed in her eyes. He narrowed his gaze, studying her. "Can you see me?" he questioned her.

She dipped her chin ever so slightly, and then bolted. Bayfield's feet scrambled into action. Running into the hallway, he skimmed the many faces, but not one belonged to her. She had simply vanished, or she was one more piece of the crazy-ass puzzle he was trying to put together.

Chapter 3

Neon-scribbles raced across monitors. Flashing machines beeped out Morse Code, and the faint smell of disinfectant welcomed Bayfield to the ICU. He loomed over his comatose body stretched out on a mechanical bed, fixating on the bandage cradling his entire head. His gaze shifted to a tangled loop of tubes protruding from his mouth as an IV dripped clear fluid into his veins.

Coach's eyes ping-ponged between Dr. Marcus and Dr. Yoo as he put before the two doctors, "I don't understand...why can't he breathe on his own?" He glanced at Bayfield's still body. "And why hasn't he woken up yet?"

Coach's words buzzed inside Bayfield's ears. Wasn't that the point of the surgery, to fix him? Bayfield faced the doctors, arms crossed over his chest. "Yeah, why?"

Dr. Yoo's expensive gray suit peeked out from beneath his white coat. He stood with his fingers laced, and used a soft-spoken tone as he explained, "The ventilator allows his body to rest so it can heal. It also maintains oxygen in the blood and keeps the pressure down inside his brain."

Coach's gaze grew distant. "I don't think that answered my questions."

Dr. Marcus stepped forward, towering a foot taller than Dr. Yoo. "Jonathan's breathing is extremely labored." He gestured to his colleague. "As Dr. Yoo pointed out, with the ventilator breathing for him, it aids in his healing process. As for the second half of your question, recovery from a TBI varies based on the individual and the brain injury."

"TBI?" Coach questioned.

"Traumatic Brain Injury," Dr. Marcus clarified.

Again, Coach eyed the pair. "In other words, you don't know when he'll wake?"

Dr. Yoo revealed the hard truth. "We don't. Recovery can be months, even years."

Coach sucked in a few deep breaths before uttering, "No."

Bayfield cocked his head. Had he said *years*?

Dr. Marcus squeezed Coach's shoulder. "Don't think ahead. Each day is a new day. Small victories."

Coach cleared his throat, offering Dr. Marcus a quick nod. "You're right."

"No, he's not!" Bayfield shouted, waving an arm in the air. "I can't stay trapped in this...this invisible limbo, or whatever the hell it is. Somebody needs to fix this!"

"I can fix it," a female voice purred into his right ear.

Bayfield swatted at his ear and stumbled back a step, before crooking his head and catching a glimpse of the female intruder. A crown of gray braids coiled about her head, growing thicker as they cascaded down her shoulders. She stood inches from him, her yellowish, cat-like orbs colliding with his. "Jesus." He squeezed his eyes shut, then popped them wide open. Taking in her translucent skin etched with black veins, he barked out a laugh. "No way. Now I'm seeing shit."

Her bloodless lips spread into a grin. "I am very much real, and someone who can help you."

His gaze darted to Coach, Dr. Marcus, and Dr. Yoo, still engrossed in conversation. Her sudden appearance hadn't triggered the slightest flicker of concern in any of them. *Gotta be stuck in some crazy-ass dream.* He slapped one cheek, and then the other. "Wake up!"

"This is not a dream, and I think you know that."

He pointed at her and claimed, "You're not real."

"I am."

"Then why can't they see you?"

She fingered the skeleton key hanging around her neck as she revealed, "I am not in the realm of the living."

"But I'm not dead."

"Correct. However,"—she paused to smirk—"your soul has stepped outside of its body and into my kingdom."

He squinted. "Kingdom?"

"Yes. My world."

His squint hardened as he dissected the tiny bolts connecting the tarnished metal framing her body. Like Frankenstein, the rivets protruded a hair above her skin's surface. The armor wasn't armor at all, it was part of her, like flesh. He swallowed hard, suffocating a gasp before it exposed his fear. "Wha—What are you?"

Her vertical-slit pupils constricted. "A collector of souls."

"A collector of souls?"

She thrust her armored shoulders back. "Yes."

He held onto his composure a second more before releasing a pent-up breath. "Time out. I'm losing my shit here. There's no way any of this is real. You're not even a person."

She let her shoulders roll into a relaxed pose. "I believe we have already established the fact that I am real, that all of this is real, and I *can* help you."

His heart seemed to freeze, then pound. More barks of laughter escaped him as he pressed his fingertips into his temples. "If this is real, I'm beyond help."

"At least hear me out."

"Hear out some creature with cat-like eyes and armor for skin?" He pursed his lips and shot her a wild-eyed look. "Why the hell not?"

The fluorescent lights bounced off her armor as she glided across the floor toward his body lying in the hospital bed. Her translucent finger tapped the ventilator. "This is keeping your body alive, yet sometimes, doctors lose faith in their machines."

He drew his brows together. "What are you saying?"

"I have seen it happen more often than not." She gave a slow shake of her braided head. "Doctors say there is no hope. Family members give up. Life support ends." Her yellowish orbs landed on him. "In circumstances like yours, when life support ends, the body breathes its last breath and the soul...well, is left behind to wander earth, alone."

No hope...family members...life support, fluttered through his mind before his brain journeyed back. *He had been thirteen. A narrow hospital hallway, reeking of cleaner, with chairs lining one side, grew clear in his mind's eye. He and Coach had claimed two of those chairs, their gazes locked on the pale-green emergency room doors. He had sat completely still with bloodstained hands lying limp in his lap. The whoosh of the doors pushing open had jerked his body out of the chair. Coach had risen to stand next to him. Two doctors appeared, but had stopped to exchange words before making their approach. As he had stared into their hollow, flat, morose expressions, Coach gripped his shoulder. The gruesome, dark words, "Mr. Bayfield has died. Mrs. Bayfield is brain dead" had ricocheted against his brain.*

Bayfield pushed that earth-shattering day far from his mind and rushed back to the present. "I can't believe I'm saying this, especially since I'm not even sure you're real, but you might have a point."

"Of course I have a point. More importantly, I can prevent your demise."

He jerked his head back. "Whoa, slow down. No one mentioned anything about dying." He sized up the determination carved into Dr. Marcus and Dr. Yoo's brows, then glanced at Coach, gripping the space of his shirt right over his heart. No way was he letting go. "No one looks like they're throwing in the towel. Maybe your spidey senses are off."

She offered him a bemused smile. "Where are my manners? I have not introduced myself." She stuck out her translucent hand. "I am Drara, forged from an inferno of magic, and brought forth with the sole purpose of governing human souls."

Bayfield's hair lifted from the nape of his neck as he digested her words. He gawked at her open palm, stalling. He didn't want to accept it, but the gnawing desire to confirm she was real burned inside his stomach. He inched his hand forward, depositing it into hers. A subtle warmth surrounded his fingers. She *was* real! He jerked away. "Did I do something wrong?"

She angled her brows into a deep frown. "What do you mean?"

He swallowed hard, then cleared his throat. "I'm not trying to offend or piss you off, but you don't look like the type of...um...*person*, that shows up before sending someone off to heaven, if you know what I mean."

She flattened her lips, letting out a huff. "As you pointed out, you are not dead. This is not judgment day. I am here to ensure the safety of your soul, nothing more."

"And just how are you going to do that?" He widened his eyes and waved his hands. "What's your master plan?"

She dusted his sarcasm off her armor as she replied, "You are skeptical, I get that. But when your soul has no body to return to, then where will you go? What will you do?" She gave a nod toward the doctors and Coach." You say they are not throwing in the towel, but not once have they broken from their conversation to look upon your body, lying there, so still. You should accept my offer."

"What exactly is your offer? I don't recall you stating it."

"You are correct, I have not," she agreed. "It is quite simple, really. I plant a seed of hope inside of their brains."

Bayfield lobbed an impatient huff her way. "Plant a seed? Sounds pretty flimsy to me."

Drara leveled her gaze at him, arching a single brow. "It appears you are the type who requires details." She stuck out her hand, waving it faster and faster in a tight circle. Ashen vapors hissed beneath the tiled floor, drifting upward and surrounding her hand. She unleashed a forceful breath, scattering the vapors. As they cleared, they unveiled an oversized book resting on her open palms. "My book of souls."

His eyes took in the book, one unlike any he'd ever seen. Intricate grooves carved into its tattered, leather-bound surface formed a raised skull dead center. Straps crafted from some kind of reptilian skin secured the six-inch thick book, as well as a tarnished bronze lock on the bottom right corner. His gaze darted to the skeleton key dangling around her neck, his mouth hanging slack. He tried to form words, yet his brain refused.

Drara felt stronger, taller, as she slipped the key into the lock, twisting it counterclockwise, and flipped the book wide open. A grayish-brown tinge flawed the once cream-colored pages cluttered with names. "Blood is the seed—your blood. I need only a few drops to craft my elixir, which I must inject into your IV. Thereafter, the elixir will flow through your veins, releasing a trace amount through your pores if anyone should approach, like an animal in fear. Once inhaled, one cannot comprehend any thoughts of failure or abandon hope." A confident smile came to her lips. "Machines stay on. Doctors continue treatment. Everyone is happy."

"Except me," he blurted out. "Am I supposed to hang out at the hospital 24/7 until someone gets it right and cures me?"

Her smile spread even widener. "Protecting your body is only the first half of my offer." She held up the book, inching it closer. "Observe these names. What do you see?"

He skimmed over the handwritten names. The red ink appeared crusted, faded, uneven. "I don't know...am I supposed to see something?"

"Look again."

Bayfield heaved a sigh, giving the page a good squint. Tiny drops of red hovered about several names—some had stains, and some splatters. His gaze bounced back and forth between them before the substance registered in his brain. "Is that blood? Are their names written in blood?"

"Yes," she answered in a matter-of-fact manner. "And yours will be too."

"Whoa, wait a minute." He held his hand up and backed away. "I haven't agreed to anything."

"It is not as menacing as it sounds, and once your name is written, it binds you to its magic and benefits."

"Benefits?"

A gleam flickered inside her eyes as she rushed out her words. "Yes! While your body lies here, your soul is transported to my mansion. Within its mystical walls, you may eat, drink, and be merry, as you humans say."

He regarded her with a narrowed gaze. "You're saying I won't be invisible inside this house? That I'll be, like, normal again?"

"Yes. And there are others there as well. You will not be alone."

As Bayfield digested her words, he caught a glimpse of Dr. Marcus and Dr. Yoo slipping out the door, leaving Coach alone. Coach's shoulders hung low, like an old man, as he stared at a spot on the floor. Bayfield turned to Drara. "If I put my arm around him, will he know I'm here?"

She shrugged. "It is hard to say. Some humans have a gift, a sixth sense if you will, which allows them insight into other realms. You can try."

Coach sagged into a chair next to Bayfield's hospital bed, blew out a long, low breath, then patted Bayfield's motionless hand. "I'm here, buddy. I'm not going anywhere."

Bayfield knelt by Coach's side, his arm suspended in air. He let it drop twice before gathering the moral fiber to hold the man who had given him everything after his parents had died, and kept giving until this very day. The man who had become his father, his only family. He clung to Coach, shuddering, as tears streamed down his cheeks.

Coach sat still, eyes fixed on the body in the hospital bed before him, his arms limp at his sides.

Bayfield jerked to his feet, brushing away tears. He was an outsider looking in on his own life. Could he stand in the background day in and day out, witnessing Coach suffer by his bedside, hoping for a miracle? A willingness to put himself in harm's way for emotional relief brushed the wall of his brain. He clenched his hands into fists and spun around to face Drara.

"Let's do this. Where do I sign?"

Chapter 4

Arielle Robbins stood at the foot of the narrow hospital bed, gazing down at her still body, littered with tubes. The low hum of machines buzzed inside her ears as she yanked a hand through her hair, twisting out the last of the ocean's saltwater. The man standing at her side, flaunting his spiffy tuxedo and top hat, had some explaining to do. "Who are you again?"

He took off his top hat, sandy-brown hair falling loose, and bowed. "Miss Robbins, as I have said, my name is Jekins."

"Well, Jekins, enlighten me. How is it that you can see and hear me when others can't?"

His gray-blue eyes twinkled. "Ah, the gift of my psychic senses, my dear."

"Psychic senses?"

Jekins gave her a wink. "Yes. To be precise: seeing, hearing, sensing, feeling, smelling, tasting, and knowing."

Arielle smirked. "Well, aren't you special."

"I am indeed," Jekins replied, brushing his knuckles across his shoulder. "Whether you believe me or not, I'm here on Drara's behalf. I have a task to fulfill, bringing you to her palace."

Arielle didn't let up. "So, you're like her chauffeur or something?"

Jekins presented her his most pleasing smile. "Among many other things, yes."

She huffed and rolled her coffee-colored eyes. "I'm trapped in a storybook nightmare. I signed Catwoman's creepy book." She nudged Jekins's shoulder. "The Mad Hatter's taking me to some mystical palace, where I'll probably turn into a tinkling fairy, spreading fairy dust over the world."

His hands briefly clenched. "No need for sarcasm. No one forced you to sign."

Arielle's chin trembled, choking out her words. "L—Look around. Do you see anyone at m—my bedside?" She launched a long, pained look toward Jekins before hanging her head. "The only one fighting for my life is me. My parents will be halfway around the world before they realize I fell off their damn yacht. I had to sign."

In a gentle tone, he put forth words he knew she'd want to hear. "You're not alone. There are many others like you. You will find comfort at Drara's palace, I'm sure of it. In fact, we must be on our way, but first, I have one more soul to collect. He is nestled on this very floor of the hospital. A roomy of sorts."

She gave Jekins a hard squint, mulling over whether or not to trust him. He was one odd character inside her mondo bizzaro situation. She pointed two V-sign fingers at her eyes before swinging them around, aiming them at Jekins's eyes. "I'm not one hundred percent certain you're sincere. Just so you know, I'm watching you."

He spread his lips into a toothy grin. "I wouldn't have it any other way, my dear."

"Fine. Lead the way."

Jekins bowed as he waved her through the doorway and into the stark hallway of the ICU. Other than the quiet hum of the machines, Arielle and Jekins claimed the hallway to themselves. Jekins strode along, swinging his arms and whistling.

"Can you tone it down a little?"

"Ah, yes, not the most appropriate behavior for someone in your situation," he offered up.

"Ya think?"

"Apologies." He pointed up ahead. "That's our stop, 403, second door on the right." He slowed his pace and peeked into the room, eyeing Coach. Bayfield stood to the side, arms folded across his chest. Jekins ducked out of view. "I didn't expect anyone to be in his room." He locked eyes with Arielle. "I can't go in there. I'll be seen. You'll have to go in and ask him to come out. His name is Jonathan."

Arielle shrugged. "Why not?" Her bare feet padded softly against the floor as she entered. She stood still for a moment, gazing at Bayfield and Coach, wishing she'd had that with her parents, but the second they could, they'd shipped her off to some far away boarding school. Money was their true baby. A haze settled in her eyes, taking her back to that prison-like fortress of a school.

It was Christmas Eve, and most of her classmates had already been picked up by their loving parents. She'd laid on her bed, clutching a teddy bear, and stared up at the drab-colored ceiling, waiting. Her parents hadn't showed. Her eyes burned with tears as she chucked Teddy across the room. She bolted after the stuffed bear and pressed him against her chest, sobbing into his fur. "T–Their n–not coming, Teddy! Th–They don't l–love me. I'm going to be alone on Christmas! What kid spends Christmas alone?" Her red, swollen eyes looked down at her bear. "Unwanted ones." As the memory faded, Arielle sucked in a painful breath, drawing Bayfield's attention.

He did a double take. "It's you."

"In the flesh." Arielle scrunched up her brows. "Well, kind of."

He turned to Coach, who took no notice of the young woman in cutoff shorts, bikini top, and bare feet, standing just inside the doorway. Bayfield cut his gaze back to her. "You're like me, aren't you?"

"If you mean no one can see or hear me, then yes."

Bayfield stepped closer to her. "What the hell is going on?"

She pursed her lips. "Your guess is as good as mine, but I need you to come out into the hallway. There's someone here for us."

His eyes narrowed. "You signed that book too?"

"Catwoman's creepy book? Yes, I had to."

Bayfield rubbed a hand across his mouth as he shook his head. "I sure wish I could figure all this out."

Arielle backed through the doorway as she waved him forward. "Well, it's not going to get any easier."

As Bayfield entered the hallway, his eyes landed on the tall man sporting a tuxedo and top hat. He shuffled back a step, barking out, "Who the hell are you?"

Arielle gave Jekins a nod. "The Mad Hatter."

Jekins tossed Arielle his most annoyed glare before reaching out his hand to Bayfield. "My name is Jekins. I'm here to take you and Miss

Robbins to Drara's palace." He paused before gesturing toward Arielle, then Bayfield. "Arielle Robbins, meet Jonathan Bayfield."

They gave each other a half-hearted nod of acknowledgment. Bayfield's gaze circled back to Jekins, sizing him up. "Not happening. For all I know, you could be just another dude trapped inside this jacked-up freakshow."

Arielle smirked. "I called it a storybook nightmare."

Bayfield tilted his head side to side, considering her choice of words. "Either way, I need reassurance that you're who you say you are before I go anywhere with you."

"I assure you, I am who I say I am," Jekins explained.

"No offense,"—Bayfield rooted his feet to the floor—"but I'm not just going to take your word for it."

Jekins took in a deep breath as he surveyed his surroundings. A group of nurses gathered at their station caught his eye. "Ha!" Jekins stretched out a finger in their direction. "I will simply walk over to these nurses and engage. You will see that they will return my conversation."

"No!" Bayfield blurted out. "Right now, the only person I know is real is sitting at my bedside. If he responds to you, then you've got a deal, and I'll go with you."

Arielle offered Bayfield a thumbs-up. "Smart."

Jekins straightened his tie. "Very well." With long strides, he entered Bayfield's room, as Arielle and Bayfield took stock from the doorway. "Excuse me, sir. I visit with the families of ICU patients to see if they need anything. Would you like some coffee or tea?"

Coach looked up and raised his brows at the man's attire before shaking his head. "Thank you, but no. I'm fine."

"Very well." Jekins bowed his head and quietly slipped out of the room, returning to his skeptics, sprouting a Cheshire cat grin. "Have I satisfied your concerns?"

"I'm good," Arielle conveyed with a quick nod.

Bayfield considered it a bit longer, pressing his lips into a fine line while studying Jekins with narrowed eyes. He wasn't sure if he trusted him, but he was a man of his word. "Yes, you have." His gaze cut to

Coach. "I need a minute to say goodbye." He didn't wait for a reply before hurrying to Coach's side and kneeling beside him. He rested his head on Coach's shoulder. "I'm going away for a while, but it's for a good reason, I think."

Coach didn't flinch, his eyes locked on Bayfield's damaged body.

Bayfield swiped at his eyes. "Anyway, um…I–I love you. Don't give up on me. Don't let the doctors give up on me. I'm fighting to beat this thing."

Jekins nudged Arielle forward. "Go make sure this doesn't take too long. We've got to get going."

"Have a heart, asshole," she mumbled, shooing him away. She crept into Bayfield's room and stood off to the side, her gaze drifting toward Bayfield's motionless body, with an octopus of tubes surrounding him, just like her. Her breaths came quicker, and she couldn't force herself to look away.

"Boxing match," Bayfield said in her ear.

She jumped as a gasp flew out of her mouth. "You scared me… what?"

"Sorry, didn't mean to." He glanced down at his body. "My opponent slammed his skull into mine. I went down and never woke up." He faced her. "At least, that's what they say. I don't remember any of it."

"I'm in a room just down the hall, looking similar." Her voice was barely a whisper as she added, "Boating accident. Got hit in the head and fell overboard." She laughed. "A fishing boat found me. Probably saved my life. At least, I hope so."

Bayfield rested his hand on her shoulder. "You're going to make it. We both are."

Her big, coffee-colored eyes gazed up at him. "Promise?"

He offered her a kind smile. "I promise."

Chapter 5

Jekins whisked Jonathan and Arielle away from the hospital inside his ebony Mercedes, complements of Drara. He peeked in his rearview mirror at Drara's latest collection of souls occupying his back seat. What a pair they were. Both were young and attractive—one clad in boxer's shorts, the other in cutoff shorts. Jekins smirked as a thought occurred to him: *well, it is come as you are.* "You two comfy back there?"

Arielle lobbed a sarcastic, "Peachy," Jekins's way, then offered him an exaggerated thumbs-up.

Bayfield furrowed his brow at her, before making eye contact with Jekins in the rearview mirror. "We're good."

Jekins nodded, letting his gaze linger on his passengers. After a moment, the road once again became his focus.

Bayfield eyed Arielle as his brain struggled to comprehend how she could remember the accident that led her to the hospital when his was a mystery. Were there levels to this realm they were trapped in? Did she have one up on him?

Arielle returned the scrutiny. "Why are you staring at me like that?"

As Arielle's voice broke through his thoughts, Bayfield blinked, then narrowed his eyes. "So, you remember everything? Your accident—I mean, how you got here?"

"Some." Her voice grew flat. "I remember it had just turned midnight, my twenty-first birthday."

Bayfield clutched her forearm. "This happened on your birthday?"

She nodded. "I'd snatched a bottle of champagne from the galley to salute the big 2-1. Stupid move, getting wasted on a boat." She exhaled, releasing the guilt. "I tripped, whacked my head, then everything got blurry. But I remember hitting the water. When I came to, I was on the fishing boat, staring down at my body."

He squeezed her arm and softly said, "Happy birthday."

Laughter burst from her lips, which quickly morphed into tears. She fanned her face, sucking in a few deep breaths. "Sorry. You're the first person to wish me that."

He scooted closer to wrap an arm around her. "Don't be sorry. It's okay."

She rested her head on his shoulder. "Thank you."

"Does anyone on the boat that you fell off of know you're missing? Are they looking for you?"

Arielle closed her eyes. "I don't know."

"What about the hospital? Do they know who you are?"

She patted the pockets of her shorts. "Didn't exactly come with ID, but with the luxuries of technology, the cops identified me through my fingerprints. "She glanced up at him and forced a smile. "The boys in blue and I have had a few run-ins."

Bayfield let his eyes grow wide. "Really? You seem so...I don't know...not the type?"

Arielle pushed herself upright. "It's nothing bad. I mean, I haven't, like, killed anyone. Just hotwired a few cars."

He jerked his head back. "Grand theft auto?"

She waved him away. "If it pisses off my parents, I'll do it. You're lucky you have a dad that cares."

"He's not my dad," Bayfield corrected. "My parents were killed in a car accident. Coach is my godfather and took me in."

She cringed. "Me and my big mouth. I'm so sorry."

It was Bayfield's turn to wave her away. "It happened a long time ago, and Coach *is* like a father to me." He looked directly at her. "You're right, though—I am lucky."

Arielle slouched into the seat, then faced the window, brushing a tear from her cheek. Off in the distance, jagged mountain tops monopolized the dark sky. They drew her attention, standing tall and proud underneath the buttery moon. A flicker of color flashed between them, pushing her to the edge of her seat.

Bayfield slid closer. "What is it?"

She pointed. "I thought I saw something between those mountains."

Bayfield peered over her shoulder, following the line of her finger. A steep, boxy, mansard roofline broke through the scattered gray clouds. "Looks like a rooftop."

"Drara's palace," Jekins clarified. "Fifty-six thousand square feet awaits."

Arielle's mouth fell open. "Fifty-six thousand square feet!"

Bayfield huffed. "But is it real, or just another illusion inside this whole mess?"

"It's very real," Jekins confirmed, tilting his head to the side. "With a touch of Drara's flair."

"Flair?"

Jekins bit the inside of his cheek. He should have left that part out. Now he had to elaborate. "Her magic lives inside its walls, allowing you folks to become whole again."

Arielle crossed her arms and shot Jekins a look. "I don't like the sound of that."

Bayfield didn't let up. "She did mention the magic, but how exactly does it work?"

Jekins returned his attention to the road. "Everything will be explained once you're there."

"Explain it to me *now*."

Jekins gripped the steering wheel. Was this kid a boxer or a lawyer? "I can't. I've only been inside the house once, when I purchased it for Drara."

Bayfield scooted forward and gripped the back on Jekins's seat. "When was that?"

"Forty years ago."

"This has been going on for forty years?" Bayfield threw at Jekins.

Jekins's mind drifted back, recalling the day he'd met Drara. *He had traveled the world with his makeshift family of eccentric carnival misfits. On that very day, he'd been reading the weathered and wrinkled palm of an old man seated at his table. A light breeze lifted the curtain to his booth, and he'd mumbled, "A closed curtain means I'm busy. Wait outside, and I'll come get you when I'm done."*

"I will not," a female voice had affirmed.

The defiance jerked his head upright. A crown of gray braids and a pair of yellowish, cat-like orbs had collided with his. Observing the black veins etched into her translucent skin, he'd given her a slight nod. "Impressive."

She'd blinked. "You are not frightened of me?"

Jekins had paused in his reply, and instead, released the old man's hand. "I see nothing more. Now, be on your way."

"Thank you." The old man had laid a twenty-dollar bill on the table. He'd passed the Frankenstein-like creature on his way out, never once glancing in her direction.

Jekins had gestured toward the empty chair. "Have a seat."

She'd lowered herself into the chair.

"To answer your question, no. I'm a freak of nature myself." He'd smirked. "As my grandmother had always said, 'The unearthly realm is at our back door. We can't close our eyes to it.'"

"Your grandmother was wise."

"Yes, she was. Now, what can I do for you?"

She'd looked to the floor as she'd said, "My human has died. I need another one."

Muffled voices shattered Jekins's thoughts, calling him back to the present. He gave his head a quick shake.

"Hey, Jekins!" Bayfield yelled for the third time. "Snap out of it!"

"He's psychic. Maybe he's having a vision," Arielle offered up in an uncertain tone.

Jekins heaved a sigh. "I'm not having a vision. I was remembering a nostalgic moment." He glanced at Bayfield. "In response to your question, it's been going on much longer. I'm just one of many who have served Drara."

"How many people are at this so-called palace?" Arielle demanded of Jekins.

"Like I said, I haven't been inside."

She put it another way. "Then how many were there when you purchased it?"

"I purchased an empty mansion, had it fully furnished, then never set another foot inside."

Bayfield butted in, "But you drop people off."

"Yes."

"So, over the forty years, how many?" Arielle repeated.

Jekins gave a half-hearted shrug. "I wasn't keeping track."

"Like ten, twenty, fifty?" Bayfield pressed.

Jekins waved a hand through the air. "Fine! Two hundred, more or less."

Bayfield and Arielle slid back in their seats, mental numbness setting in.

Jekins caught sight of his dumbfounded passengers in the rearview mirror. He'd seen those same slacken mouths and unfocused gazes many times before when he'd delivered unsettling news. He was used to it, they weren't. In his most uplifting, positive tone, he offered them some hope. "Drara is very sympathetic toward the souls who have signed her book. She is aware of what a disheartening experience this can be. Give her palace a chance. It may surprise you."

Bayfield held up a hand, warding off Jekins. "I'm not ready to surrender just yet. I'm a visual person. I have to see it to believe it."

Arielle tucked her hands behind her elbows and offered Jekins a small smile. "I don't know what to think anymore."

Jekins gave a nod toward the approaching street—Northhollow Lane. "You won't have to wait long." He veered the car right, shifting into low gear before climbing the steep, narrow road.

Drara's palace sat at the very top. The French style mega mansion, with its gray-blue roofline and many cream-colored archways, stretched out on 2.5 acres of land. Rows of windows lined the front exterior—an irresistible temptation for sunlight to flood each room.

A blanket of greenery, mature trees, and three fountains surrounding the motor court welcomed its newest arrivals as Jekins pulled up to the grand entrance. He didn't bother to cut the engine as he jumped out of the car and pulled the back passenger door open. "This is where I say farewell. Have fun storming the castle!"

Bayfield forced a smile. "It's been real." He turned away from Jekins and offered Arielle his hand.

She scooted across the seat to accept it. As her feet touched the ground, a thought occurred to her, creasing her brow. She glanced at the house, and then Jekins. Arielle latched onto Jekins's arm, stopping him. "Tell me why you've never gone back inside. Is it because you won't or can't?"

Bayfield crossed his arms, locking eyes with Jekins. "I'd like to know too."

Jekins's gaze darted between Bayfield and Arielle. A few seconds drifted by before he answered. "I ca—"

Arielle didn't let him finish, demanding, "Why can't you?"

Jekins drew in a breath and released it before speaking. "A soul that steps through the door receives a carbon copy of its body. A body that steps through the door will lose its soul."

Chapter 6

Under the starlit sky, Bayfield and Arielle faced the front door, centered inside a massive archway. Its columns blocked beams of moonlight and cast a dark shadow over the entryway.

Arielle squinted at the opaque glass and pursed her lips, trying to catch a glimpse of whatever was on the other side. She glanced at Bayfield. "Should we knock?"

A wrinkle of doubt inched across his forehead. Shaking off the foreboding, he answered, "Screw it. We're walking in." He gave the giant bronze handle a good push.

The sophisticated iron frame swung wide open, exposing a vacant, stark-white foyer, adorned with polished marble floors in bold black trim. The quiet rang through their ears—a warning to stay away, or a cordial gesture to enter? As they crossed the threshold, the door closed, shutting out the outside world.

Arielle tilted her head. "That was a little creepy."

Bayfield shrugged. "Probably got it hooked up to a motion sensor." His eyes traced the black railing, up one side and down the other of the grand stairway, leading to the second floor. "Man, this place had to cost some bucks."

Arielle gave the room a nod of approval. "My parents are filthy rich, but this place makes them look dirt poor."

A gooey, sticky, splashing sound echoed off the walls.

Arielle let out a shriek. "What was that?" She spun around and faced the staircase. The squishy sound, like waterlogged rainboots, intensified. She squinted, searching for the source of the sound, yet an empty foyer filled her vision.

Bayfield flinched as the swishing sound neared his face. "I can't see anything. Can you?"

The splashing grew louder, stronger, before hurling a soggy, gummy substance over her. "It's on me!" The wet, sticky mess slid down her flesh, coiling around every inch of her body.

"That shit's on me too!"

A heaviness affected her limbs, molding her into a stationary piece of the foyer. Her lips struggled to form words as she mumbled, "Now I can't move!"

"Me neither," Bayfield grinded out through clenched teeth. Every muscle strained under his skin as he fought the force constricting him.

At the height of alarm, the peaceful silence returned to the foyer. The invisible constraints adhered to their flesh released, restoring movement to their limbs. Bayfield turned in all directions, searching for the ambiguous force.

Arielle shuddered, then brushed at the goose bumps on her arms. Her skin felt different: denser, fleshier, real. "Wait!"

Bayfield jerked his head in her direction, his bodyweight thrusting him forward. He felt 200 pounds again, the featherlight feeling gone. "I think..." He looked himself over, furrowing his brows. "I think we just got our bodies back."

Footsteps approached, belonging to a young man clad in ripped jeans, T-shirt, and flip-flops, halting any reply from Arielle. His mop of curly black hair bounced as he trekked down the stairs. "Wassup." He high-fived Bayfield, then Arielle. "I'm Tommy, gate keeper of this shindig. You must be Jonathan and Arielle, the new kids on the block. And before you ask, Jekins hits me up with a text on my newbies." He nodded toward the stairs. "Your rooms await. You can grab a shower, change, then come downstairs for some grub."

"A shower? Oh my God! I can finally get this sea water stench out of my hair."

Bayfield didn't budge, and blocked Arielle's path with his arm. "Whoa, hang on." He pointed a finger over his shoulder. "What the hell just happened back there? I need information."

Tommy chuckled. "I'll give you the 411 as we walk." Again, he gestured toward the stairs. "C'mon."

Arielle touched Bayfield's forearm. "Decompress a little. We did sign the book, so..."

Bayfield's lips straightened into a firm line. "Fine."

Tommy gave a quick nod. "Okay, then. Follow me."

Tommy hiked the stairs two at a time, escorting the latest members onto the second floor. The stark-white color and black trim continued throughout, with the marble flooring spanning into the hallway. "Got a ways to travel before we land at your digs. Little info on the palace—two levels and one killer basement." He flashed a smile. "It's decked out with a theater, bar lounge, bowling alley, gym, and indoor pool, the works. If you're interested, tonight's eighties night in the bar lounge."

"Eighties?" Arielle raised her brow. "You do know it's 2019, right?"

"Not everyone here is a Gen Z. Gotta account for all generations."

A warm glow brightened Bayfield's expression. "Coach blasted eighties music nonstop. I couldn't get away from the stuff. Know it by heart."

Tommy clapped him on the back. "You should check it out later."

"Yeah, maybe, but I'm more interested—"

"In how you got your body back," Tommy finished for him. "In truth, you didn't. It's a carbon copy, a loaner if you will. Fits like a glove right over your soul."

Bayfield lifted a single brow, and Arielle rolled her eyes, responding with, "Let me guess, fairy dust?"

Tommy wagged a finger at her. "You're not far off. It's Drara's magic."

"If we're stuck here, how do we check on our real bodies?" Arielle inquired.

"You can come and go as you please." Tommy held up his hand, predicting Arielle's next question. "There's more."

Bayfield crossed his arms. "There always is."

Tommy waved away the sarcasm before continuing. "No matter how many times you reenter, Drara's magic will produce a carbon copy for your soul. But on the flip side, every time you walk out that door, the atmosphere senses an imposter."

"And...?" Bayfield urged.

"It rips the simulation apart." He grimaced. "Hurts like a son of a bitch too. That's why most of us stay put."

Arielle touched the base of her throat, swallowing hard. "Well, that's comforting."

Bayfield gave the warning little consideration. "We'll see."

"I was like you—had to see for myself," Tommy snickered. "Come find me after you give it a try, and I'll say I told you so." He stopped in between two doors on opposite sides of the hallway, each displaying a name plate. "Ah, here we are. Jonathan, you're on the left, and Arielle, you're on the right." He rubbed his hands together. "What else? Oh yeah, there's a call button in your rooms. Give it a push when you're ready to come downstairs. I'll come back and take you on the grand tour. Any questions?"

Bayfield had a ton, but to quote Tommy, he was a "see for yourself" kind of guy. *One breakout coming right up.* "No questions."

Arielle chewed on her bottom lip, her brain on overload. Concentration was impossible. The one clear thing in focus was that shower. "Nope."

"Alrighty, then. Later." Tommy shoved his hands in his pockets and sauntered down the hall.

Arielle's eyes found Bayfield's, offering him a feeble smile. "Will you wait for me? I don't want to go downstairs alone."

His smile was much more convincing. "Of course."

"Give me about a half hour?"

"Half hour it is."

She fluttered her fingers in a waving fashion, then closed herself off inside the room. A pallet of beige inhabited the four walls; furniture, drapery, and accent pieces blended together like a painting around her. Her gaze fell upon a king size bed occupying the center wall, adorned with a taupe canopy and countless pillows. Arielle ran her fingers along the satin comforter as she drifted past the bed toward a small sitting area. Jogger pants, white tank, pink duster, slip-on sneakers, and a bra and panties were deliberately draped over the chaise, facing a bay window.

All her absolute faves, yet how had they known her style? In the far corner of the room, two open doorways beckoned her to enter. She gathered up the clothes and pursued the invitation.

She peeked inside the first door, revealing a walk-in closet. Ripped jeans, dusters, oversized sweaters, graphic tees, boots, and sneakers lined the long, narrow room. She turned in a circle, mouth slacken, eyes wide, gawking at the exact replica of her own closet at home. A shiver crawled over her flesh and she rubbed it away, dropping the clothes in a pile on the floor. "They're stalkers." She scooped up the clothes and slammed the door shut.

Door number two, the master bath, gave off a far less creepy vibe, with a free-standing tub dead center, a massive marble vanity claiming the center wall, and a shower, taking up real estate on the opposing wall, with dual rainfall heads, all remaining faithful to the beige color pallet. Arielle flipped the shower lever upward, blasting hot water. Delicious warm steam swirled about her as she stepped inside the glass shower and underneath the downpour, washing away the hopelessness of the last two days.

With freshly shampooed hair and skin, Arielle faced herself in the oval mirror. The thought of never escaping this place began to overwhelm her, but she quickly pushed it out of her mind with a purposeful shudder. Stepping into her clothes, she threw her damp hair into a messy bun. She gave her reflection a nod of approval, then hurried off to team up with Bayfield for the enlightening house tour.

****

Bayfield waited outside his room, leaning against the wall, muscular arms crossed, sporting a pair of faded blue jeans, black T-shirt, and high-top leather sneakers. As Arielle appeared, he set his sights on her, offering her a wide smile. "I like your style."

Arielle held her breath as a willingness to believe that everything would be alright flooded her with warmth. He, Jonathan, had done that. A beaming expression touched her face. "You aren't so bad yourself."

They took another moment to look each other over before their gazes darted to opposite walls of the hallway.

Bayfield broke the awkward silence. "Did you press the call button?"

"Crap. I forgot."

"I'll get it." Bayfield slipped into his room and came back with a thumbs-up. "I guess we wait."

Arielle shrugged. "I guess so." She scrunched her brows together, recalling the weird wardrobe moment. "Hey, did you notice anything mondo bizarro in your room?"

"The room, no." He gestured to his outfit. "But the clothes in the closet, hell to the yes. Looked like my closet at home. Eerie. But what hasn't been jacked-up about this whole thing?" He snapped his fingers. "Oh yeah, and I noticed that trippy copper sheen affecting our eyes is now gone."

She pursed her lips, not ready to let the clothing thing go. "How did they know, though? Did they raid our bedrooms? Have they been stalking us? Were our accidents really accidents?"

Bayfield rested his hands on her shoulders, locking his eyes on hers. "Hey, don't spin out. I'm a hundred percent sure none of this was premeditated. Fate just threw us a curveball and being here gives the doctors more time to fix what's wrong. Maybe Drara and her team just want us to feel comfortable and less afraid as we wait."

Her eyes fixated on him as she drank in his words. Was he right? The knot twisting her gut told her he wasn't, but she forced a smile. "You're right, I need to chill. We'll get through this."

He squeezed her shoulders. "We will."

"Peeps, I got your call." Tommy spread his arms wide. "Ready for the grand tour?"

Arielle gave Bayfield a slight nod, and in turn, he offered her a dimpled grin. Facing Tommy, he affirmed, "We are."

Tommy snubbed the second level with a wave of his hand. "Nothing to see here but bedrooms. Let's hit the first floor. It's much more interesting." Tommy trekked forward, whistling, while Arielle and Bayfield tagged behind at a steady pace. At the bottom of the stairs, he huffed, "C'mon, folks, chop-chop. Put a little steam into it."

"What's the rush?" Arielle protested. "It's not like we've got some place to be."

"This is true." Tommy sucked in a deep breath and blew it out. "Clearing my chi."

Arielle rolled her eyes. "Oh my God."

Bayfield took his sights off Arielle and focused on Tommy. "Show us whatcha got."

Tommy rubbed his palms together, smiling. "Follow me." Blazing past several rooms, he rattled off the names: "Living room, formal dining, library, blah, blah, blah."

Arielle had about a half a second to peek inside each room as Tommy charged through the house. Blah was right. More of the same bland, boring beige décor. She knew expensive things, and these fabrics, accent pieces, and furnishings were high-end, probably costing thousands, but man, what a snore.

"I've got two rooms on the first floor I want to show you. You're gonna like 'em." Tommy veered right, then left, then right again, before stopping in front of a massive kitchen. The room housed the same marble floors and stark-white walls, but the cabinets were a beautiful slate-gray with a stunning herringbone mosaic backsplash to match. "The kitchen is our number one hangout room." Tommy jogged over to the fridge. "How about a cool brewski?"

Bayfield deliberately lowered his head and squinted at Tommy. "Beer? We can really drink?"

"Of course you can."

Bayfield snuck a peek at Arielle, but she only shrugged.

"Um..." Bayfield glanced about the room as if it held the answers.

Tommy added, "You can eat, drink, get some booty, take a piss, take a sh—"

Arielle cut him off. "Dude, TMI."

Tommy bellowed out in laughter. "My point is, whatever you did before the accident, you can do inside these walls."

Bayfield weighed the options, then gave his head a firm shake. "Wait, hang on. Let's say we do all those things. How will it affect our bodies back at the hospital?"

Arielle paused, conjuring up an image of her motionless body littered with tubes. "Jonathan's got a point."

"Newbies, take a breather. We're talking apples and oranges here." Tommy wagged a finger at Arielle, and then at Bayfield. "One has nothing to do with the other. There's no connection. This body is temporary, not a replacement."

Bayfield let out a deep, weighted sigh. "Since we're at a disadvantage, we'll just have to take your word for it."

Tommy offered two thumbs-up before grabbing 3 beers and setting them on the center island. He took a swig of his own, then gave a nod toward the two remaining beers. "This will help you relax."

"What the hell." Arielle reached for the beer and took a hearty swallow. "I need something to help me relax."

Bayfield's tight expression relayed he wasn't fully committed, yet accepted the bottle. "So, what's the second room?"

Tommy waved them forward. "We call it 'The Secret Garden.'"

Bayfield and Arielle zigzagged after Tommy as he escorted them through the hallway maze. At the end, he pushed open a set of double glass doors and led them into a sanctuary of greenery.

As Arielle crossed the threshold, her hand covered her mouth as she turned in a slow circle, eyes widening. Palm trees lined the walls, reaching up and spreading out beneath the glass cathedral ceiling. Plants of every shape, size, and color claimed their corners of the room. Ivory statues bathed in moonlight posed in front of the many arched windows. A curved sofa and chair, the fabric resembling stone, sat in the heart of all the foliage.

A feeling of weightlessness came over her, and she sank into the cushions of the chair, shaking her head. "It's beautiful."

Bayfield nursed his beer and gave a slight nod. "I can't complain."

Tommy grinned. "I thought you'd like it, but there's more to see. Next stop, the basement. We'll take the elevator. It's the easiest way."

"Of course it is," Bayfield mumbled under his breath.

Arielle gave one last look around, then blew a kiss into the room before nudging Bayfield's arm. "You gotta admit, that garden was crazy cool."

He cracked a smile. "It was pretty awesome, wasn't it?"

She bounced up and down on her toes. "Hell yes!"

"Did you just hop?"

Arielle erupted with laughter, swayed, then latched onto his arm, steadying herself. "I did, and it felt good!"

Bayfield struggled to suppress the glee bubbling up inside his chest, but it spewed out with force. He couldn't stop snorting, which pushed Arielle over the edge. They fell against each other, shoulder to shoulder, cackling hysterically.

"Must be the beer," Tommy offered up. "Hey, elevator's over here."

As Bayfield and Arielle reached the elevator, they shook off the giggles, staring straight-faced at the silver door. A soft chime announced its arrival before welcoming them to enter. Tommy popped in first and kept the doors from closing. Inside the mirrored walls and polished tile, Tommy punched *ground floor*. "Pull out your e-tickets and get ready to ride."

Arielle scrunched her brows together. "Huh?"

"It's a throwback from Disneyland," Bayfield pointed out, and her frown deepened. "Coach has a framed e-ticket at home. Can't count how many times I had to hear that story."

"Aw," Arielle teased.

The doors parted, silencing any reply from Bayfield. Tommy shooed them into the hallway and rattled off, "Where to? The bar lounge, twenty seat theater, bowling alley, indoor pool, fitness center, craft room, or salon?"

Bayfield blurted out, "Fitness center."

Arielle's response overlapped Bayfield's. "Salon."

Tommy wrinkled his brow. "Um, no and no. Don't you people know how to have fun?" He glanced at their empty bottles. "Obviously, a refill's in order. We're hittin' the bar." He sped off without waiting for a reply.

Bayfield threw up his hands. "What the hell?"

Arielle heaved a sigh, then pushed forward. "C'mon. Let's follow him."

Bayfield cast a narrowed gaze on Tommy. "Fine. But as soon as we can, we're ditching this guy."

"Agreed."

Chapter 7

The bar lounge, with its industrial rustic décor and concrete floors, severed the boring beige theme asserting itself throughout the mansion. Red brick walls wrapped the entire room, complementing the reclaimed wood lining the ceiling. Pendant lighting offered a warm glow over the metal bar, as well as the roaring fire crackling inside an exposed brick hearth, releasing an intoxicating scent of burning wood.

Arielle stood completely still, her eyelashes fluttering as the aroma of the many flavors of liquor spicing the air reached her nose. "Oh my God. It smells delish in here." She blinked, reverting to a conscious state, taking in the people scattered around the bar. Their voices blurred inside her head as they shouted over the alien music. She inched closer to Bayfield, then glanced at Tommy. "So, they're all like us?"

Tommy smirked. "Yep. Ready for something a little stronger than beer?"

"Brandy, straight up," Arielle rattled off.

Bayfield furrowed his brows at her. "Wow, okay." He faced Tommy. "I'll stick with beer, thanks."

Tommy wagged a finger at them. "You got it. Be back in a jiff."

Bayfield lobbed a questioning stare at Arielle. "Brandy? What's that about?"

"There's a lot of people, Jonathan. Doesn't that bother you?"

He sighed loudly. "This whole thing bothers me. And it was you who told me to decompress, remember?"

"Yeah, but..." Her gaze skimmed the many faces. "There's gotta be about fifty people here."

"Jekins already fessed up to unloading about two-hundred souls, so what gives?"

Arielle swallowed hard. "For every one of them, there's a hospital bed with a lifeless body in it. What if we're forgotten? What if we slip through the cracks?"

Bayfield took her hand and squeezed it. "We just got here. We don't know anything about these people." He jutted a hand their way. "I mean, look at them. They're laughing, singing along to the music, throwing back drinks. None of them seem upset."

"Maybe," she replied, her tone hesitant.

Tommy reemerged, two beers and a snifter of brandy cupped between his hands. "Help me out, guys."

Bayfield grabbed up a beer, then offered the snifter to Arielle. He took a swig, watching her over the rim. "You okay?"

She downed a generous swallow, shuddering as the instant warmth spread through her veins, quieting the angst. "Better."

Tommy glanced at his wristwatch, then chugged his beer, emptying it in several gulps. "Okay, you crazy kids, I'm out. Explore, have fun, shoot the shit, whatever. If you get lost, make your way back to the grand staircase. It's the central point for everything in this house."

Bayfield flinched, confused. "That's it? What about—"

Tommy raised his hand to halt him. "Rome wasn't built in a day. I'll answer more questions tomorrow, but for now, I've got other places to be. Later." He offered them a smile and sprinted toward the door.

Tension spread through Bayfield's neck. "I don't like that guy."

"He's a little weird." She glanced around the room. "Now what?"

Bayfield surveyed the crowd. "Not sure. We could—"

At that moment, two men and two women, all pushing sixty, approached them. The tallest of the four, pulling off a slick comb-over, stuck out his hand. "Name's Mitch." He gestured to the man on his right, with a full head of salt and pepper hair. "This is George." He gave a nod toward the two women on his left, both sporting the bleached blonde Marilyn Monroe look. "And these two gorgeous gals are Trixie and Candy."

A snicker trickled past Arielle's lips. *Trixie and Candy? Seriously?* She stifled the giggle with a swallow of brandy and reached for his hand. "Arielle."

"Jonathan," Bayfield replied, offering his hand as well.

"You're new here," Trixie pointed out.

"Yes," Bayfield agreed. "Arrived today."

"And the four of you?" Arielle questioned.

Mitch placed a hand on his chest. "I'm coming up on eight. George is working on five, and Trixie and Candy, three."

Arielle choked on her brandy. Bayfield patted her back, clearing the burning alcohol swimming in her throat. Her eyes doubled in size. "Years?"

A bark of laughter exploded out of Bayfield mouth. "Arielle, come on. I'm sure he meant days."

George chuckled. "No, she's right. It's years."

Bayfield shuffled back a step, a dazed look clouding his eyes. "That... That can't be true."

Arielle knocked back her brandy, then stared into the empty glass. "I think I need another."

Trixie giggled, a genuine smile on her lips. "I think a refill's in order."

Arielle swiftly handed Trixie the snifter. "Brandy, please. Thank you."

"Shot of vodka," Bayfield blurted out.

Mitch slapped Bayfield on the back. "That'll calm the nerves, son."

"We could all use a refill," Candy pointed out. "I'll help you carry 'em."

Trixie hurried off with Candy at her side, leaving Mitch and George to tend to Bayfield and Arielle.

Mitch exchanged looks with the horrified rookies. "It's not what you think." He spread his arms wide. "Look around. We have a great life here, and we want for nothing. We chose to stay."

"Are you saying you've been in a coma all this time, or the doctors weren't able to..." Arielle couldn't bring herself to finish.

Bayfield did it for her, and didn't mince words. "Save you, and you died?"

George slapped his thigh. "Good one!"

"How's that funny?"

George gathered his brows, erasing any signs of mirth. "My first few days were tough. The unknown was quite intimidating. Each day became less unsettling, and after a while, I'd found peace here, and had no desire to leave. Tommy texted Jekins with instructions to relay my wishes to Drara. How she accomplished that is of no concern to me, and *that* was three and half years ago."

Bayfield rubbed a hand over his mouth and muttered, "Jesus."

Arielle's hands trembled before clasping them together. "I don't want to be here a month, let alone years."

Mitch held his hands up in an apologetic fashion. "What George is getting at is, whatever happened on the outside doesn't matter to us. This is the life we chose, and we're fine with that. It doesn't have to be what you choose, though."

Trixie and Candy returned with drinks in hand. "We got doubles for all," Trixie chirped happily.

"Perfect timing." George snatched up Bayfield's and Arielle's, quickly handing them over to the newbies. "A swift drink will do the two of you good."

Bayfield tossed back his double shot of vodka and cringed. The burn of alcohol spread through his chest, softening his suspicions, and spread an inebriated grin on his face. The influence vanished as he caught sight of Arielle. She'd gulped half her supersized brandy, yet the haunted glaze camouflaging her beautiful coffee-brown eyes remained. The instinct to protect her erupted through his bones and pushed him forward. Bayfield wedged himself between Arielle and George, forcing her to look only at him. He flashed his best dimpled smile and whispered, "Wanna get out of here?"

Arielle locked her eyes on his as a breath of relief escaped her. "Yes."

He took her hand, then faced the gang of four. "It was great meeting you. We're gonna go explore."

George belted out, "Have fun storming the castle!"

Trixie blew them a kiss and cooed, "Take care you two."

Mitch chuckled and raised his glass, as Candy called after them, "It was nice meeting you."

Bayfield led Arielle out the door and into a vacant hallway, leaving the barflies and eighties music behind. "Which way?"

"Anywhere quiet. I need to get their words out of my head."

He ventured right. A few steps in, a digital sign dangling from the ceiling caught his attention. "Movie is in session. Do not enter." He glanced at Arielle. "Looks like we're not going to the movies."

"I'm not up for a movie. I need quiet, remember?"

Bayfield faked a bow. "Forgive me, Princess."

She shooed him away with a huff, then stopped mid-step. "Wait." She stuck her nose in the air. "I smell popcorn." A wide grin spread across her lips. "*Buttered* popcorn."

Bayfield took a whiff. "You're right."

They pursued the aroma like hounds, charging forward with laughter, before skidding to a stop in front of an old-fashioned popcorn stand and soda machine. Arielle grabbed Bayfield's arm, her face beaming. "Oh, we're so doing this."

He reached the stand first. "Extra butter is nonnegotiable."

Arielle drove the scoop into the mound of popcorn bouncing about the glass case, as Bayfield waited with his hand on the butter pump. He smothered the golden liquid over the overstuffed bag, and puffs of white landed on the floor.

Arielle cackled. "You're spilling it everywhere."

"Don't worry, there's still plenty." He flashed her a charming smile. "Soda?"

She bobbed her head in agreement. "Coke, please."

He handed her the bloated bag of popcorn dripping with butter. "Two large Cokes coming up."

Hands full, they wandered farther down the hall, shoving popcorn into their mouths and searching for a quiet place to kick back. A red neon sign flashing *Bowling, Anyone?* collided with Bayfield's vision. He hit the brakes and blurted out, "Bowling."

She wrinkled her nose. "How's that quiet? I can't run into more blue hairs, bragging about racking up years here."

Bayfield bent down to look her in the eyes. "I'll make you a deal. If there's people inside, we'll leave. If it's empty, we stay. Deal?"

"Fine."

He smirked. "I think you really might be a princess."

She huffed as he stuck his head inside the door, reporting back with a thumbs-up. "Coast it clear. Everyone must be at the bar or the movie."

Arielle sighed and followed him inside. The cobalt-blue two-lane bowling alley, complete with three flashing pinball machines, a high-end pool table, and one massive blue velvet sectional, was indeed empty.

Bayfield waved her over to the lane. "You go first."

Arielle stared at the white pins with red stripes. With both hands, she lobbed the ball forward. "Oh my God," she uttered as it hit with a thud, rolling into the gutter.

"That's okay, it happens." Bayfield scooped up a ball. "Hold the ball like this," he explained, placing his fingers inside the holes and cradling it in his palm. "Make a quick approach to the line, then let it fly."

"Got it." Following Bayfield's demo, Arielle made her second attempt. The ball rushed down the center of the lane, veered left, and landed in the gutter. She clenched her fists and shouted, "Oh, come on! I did everything right."

Bayfield patted her shoulder. "You'll get it." He seized a bright orange ball, stopped to grin over his shoulder at her, then rushed the line. The ball soared, smacking the pins dead center, knocking every single one down. He jogged in a circle, thrusting his hands in the air. "And the crowd roared."

"No way!"

"Yes way. Strike two, coming up." Bayfield made his approach, narrowing his gaze as he let the ball fly. The orange whirl whooshed down the lane, plowing into the pins with a booming crackle. "Ha!" he shouted, then patted himself on the back.

Arielle groaned. "You've got to be kidding me."

"You're up. Just relax."

She stared down the pins with determination, bolted forward, and lobbed the ball. It clobbered the wooden lane and bounced straight into the gutter—again. She threw her hands up in an "I give up" gesture.

"No, don't give up. Come on, you got this," Bayfield urged with a crisp nod.

Arielle let out an impatient huff as she picked up a ball. "I think you're enjoying this."

He tipped his head toward the lane. "Bowl."

As Arielle swung her arm back, the ball slipped, landing with a thump behind her.

Bayfield turned away, bursting into laughter.

"I'm done." She strayed from the game, snatching up her popcorn and soda before flopping down on the sectional.

Bayfield staggered after her, cackling. "You're, like, the worst bowler ever."

"Funny," she mocked.

"Okay, okay." He sucked in a few breaths, purging his humor. "I had you at a disadvantage. I'm actually a great bowler."

"I'd say."

He shrugged. "Had some anger issues after my parents died. Coach signed me up in a league."

A thoughtful expression came over her, then her gaze grew distant. "I envy what you have with Coach."

Bayfield sank into the cushions next to her, his gaze resting on her face. "Why so torqued with your parents?" He wiggled his brows. "And what's the 411 on the whole hotwiring cars thing?"

She curled her knees toward her chest and hugged them. "A share equals a share. If I spill about my parents, you have to do the same."

He offered her an understanding nod. "Fair enough."

A quiet sigh escaped her lips as wretched memories floated to the surface. A brutal one pinned itself to the walls of her brain—her twelfth birthday. *Her parents had managed to snag a table at the opening of Coral Reef, a below sea level restaurant. The narrow glass room filled* with graceful creatures of the sea swimming about had mesmerized her. Her eyes had sparkled as she shouted, "Best fishbowl ever!"

Her mother had pressed a finger to her lips. "Shhh, people are trying to enjoy their meal."

Arielle had shoved a piece of chicken into her mouth, shooting a glare her mother's way.

"Denise, cut Arielle some slack," her father had chimed in. "Everyone's oohing and aahing."

"Carey." Her mother had turned sharply, angling her body toward her father. "Behavior is everything. We aren't raising a monkey."

"I'm not a monkey," Arielle had snapped, crossing her arms.

Her mother had eyed her with that silent glare of hers, then wagged a finger at her.

Just then, a school of fish had passed by, and she'd closed her eyes, wishing she was one of them. It's not worth it pierced the bitterness swelling within Arielle's brain. How long she had remained tucked away inside her thoughts, she couldn't recall, but a sudden stillness drew her eyelids open. Empty chairs on either side of her had come into view. Her gaze had darted about, searching for her parents, and a flash of mint green on the edge of the table had caught her eye. She swallowed hard before she had slowly turned her head. Dollar bills folded inside a money clip had been placed next to her plate. Her chin trembled as she had whispered, "They left me."

Waiters had surrounded the table then, placing a piece of cake with a single flaming candle in front of her, serenading, "Happy birthday to you. Happy birthday to you. Happy birthday, happy birthday. Happy birthday to you."

Arielle shattered the miserable remembrance with a jerk of her head. She faced Bayfield, her voice cold and flat. "My parents, if you can call them that, left me with nannies until they could ship me off to boarding school. Checked in for like half my birthdays. Forgot about me on most holidays. Showed affection with money." She pursed her lips and grinded out, "So yeah, my parents are dicks. I used to be all boohoo about it, then I went section 8. Picked fights, shoplifted, snuck boys into my room, whatever would make them go mental. Got involved with a guy whose dad was a mechanic; hence the whole car thief thing." Arielle stood and curtsied. "And there you have it."

Bayfield scooted closer to her and fumbled with his words. "I—I don't...I'm so sorry, Arielle."

"You're turn."

Bayfield stared down at his hands. A streak of dark red blood blinked behind his eyelids, that horrifying day rushing back. *He couldn't believe his parents had parked the uncool sedan right in front of the school. His friends would be all over it and never let him live it down. Without saying goodbye, he'd thrown the door open and bolted, reaching the grassy area in seconds. A sudden screeching of breaks and splintering glass had ruptured his eardrums. His legs buckled. A teacher had steadied him before a stampede of shrieking people scurried in every direction. His gaze had followed the frenzy, landing on a demolished pickup truck, pinning a flattened car. Someone had screamed, "Call 911!"*

The brownish color of the pinned car burned recognition in his gut. His legs pounded the ground before his brain had even acknowledged it. A guttural shriek had blasted out of his mouth. "Mom! Dad!" In front of the crash site, he'd dropped to his knees, peering inside the car. Blood had spattered across the leather seats, windshield, dashboard, and the two crumpled bodies no longer resembled his parents. Screams had erupted from the depths of his soul as tears blurred his vision. He'd managed to get his hands inside the car and pressed them down as hard as he could over his mother's gushing neck wound. Warm blood had spurted between his fingers.

Sirens blazed off in the distance. Footsteps hammering the pavement approached, and strong hands had pulled him away. "No!" he'd cried. "Mom! Dad!"

A man dressed in blue, with a bag hung over his shoulder, had used a calm, gentle voice. "I need you to stay back and let us do our jobs. We're here to help."

"Jonathan," Arielle called out, resting her hand on his arm.

He shook his head, pulling himself away from the past and back into the present. His eyes found hers, and he offered her a faint smile. "My parents only had one car, and my mom had to do errands so she was gonna drive my dad to work and me to school because I missed the bus. I was embarrassed to have my friends see me, so as soon as they parked, I took off. I didn't even say goodbye." His voice broke. "I'm sorry."

She squeezed his arm. "It's okay. Take your time."

He clenched his jaw as he said, "Some drunk guy behind the wheel of a gigantic truck rammed into my parents' car. My parents didn't make it."

Arielle gasped. "Oh my God, I'm so sorry."

"It was my fault. If I hadn't missed the bus, they'd still be alive."

"Don't say that. You can't blame yourself."

"That's what Coach says. He helped me work all the anger and guilt out. Got me involved with all kinds of hobbies." He offered her a brighter smile. "Bowling being one of them."

She returned the smile. "Thank God for Coach."

He sniffed and wiped his nose. "He saved me, and now I'm here, and I can't even let him know."

"Do you think..." She paused, drew in a breath, then released it. "Do you think we shouldn't have signed creepy Catwoman's book?"

"That remains to be seen." He downed the last of his Coke before raising and shaking out his arms. "It's been a long emotional day. We should get some sleep."

A sense of calm wrapped around her as she gazed at him. Where would she be in all this mess without this strong boxer with the dimpled cheeks at her side? She placed a fist against her heart. "If I have to be stuck inside this three-ring circus, I'm grateful it's with you."

His dimpled smile appeared, accompanied by a rose blush flushing his cheeks. "You know that's gonna go to my head, right?"

She flashed a flirty smile and winked. "I meant for it to."

Chapter 8

The next morning, Arielle woke, sprawled out on her bed, still in the previous night's clothes. Her eyes fluttered closed as she stretched her arms overhead. "Day two," she mumbled, sitting up and swinging her legs over the side. She staggered across the room, shedding her clothes and stumbling into the shower. Hot water rained down on her for several minutes before lifting the drowsing fog. Wakefulness came with questions. How many people chose Mitch's way? Had their bodies died? Could she trust Drara at her word? Was it all a hoax? Arielle massaged her temples. "Enough already." She inhaled a calming breath before freeing her mind of the chaos and shut the water off.

Peering at her reflection in the mirror, she was unable to tell this impostor apart from her real self. Her chin trembled. "No," she pledged, holding her head high. "I will not allow tears to fall." She spun on her heels and marched into the closet. Rummaging through the clothes, she grabbed a pair of distressed skinny jeans and a graphic tee, spelling out *Because Coffee* off their hangers. A pair of Skechers completed her look. With a bounce in her step, she approached the door when a folded sheet of paper lying just inside the doorway slowed her pace. Arielle flipped it open and read it.

Good morning, Arielle. Got up early to hit the gym. Didn't want you to freak if you couldn't find me. Can't wait to see you — J.

She read the last line again. *Can't wait to see you.* Her pulse quickened, spreading a radiant glow over her skin. Fanning herself with the paper, she couldn't contain her smile. She hunted down a pen, then jotted on the back of Bayfield's note.

Morning, Jonathan. It's 8:30 a.m., and I'm heading to the kitchen. Can't wait to see you too!

She stopped at Jonathan's door. Sliding the note underneath, a famished growl rumbled through her stomach. "Okay, okay," she answered the groan, pressing her hand to her stomach.

Humming her favorite song "Wolves" and stepping lightly to its beat, Arielle headed down the grand staircase, pursuing some much-needed grub.

She followed the path from Tommy's tour, retracing his steps toward the kitchen. A whiff of Applewood bacon hovered in the air, escorting Arielle to the entryway. She crossed the threshold, pausing as her gaze glided over the room. Sunlight penetrated the floor-to-ceiling windows, flooding the stark-white kitchen with rays of natural light; a stunning attribute she'd missed the night before. Dainty bistro dining sets, garnished with fresh cut flowers, housed more guests of Catwoman. She averted her eyes—too many unknow faces to take in.

The scrumptious aroma of breakfast munchies, mixed with the undeniable smell of coffee, distracted Arielle, steering her toward the kitchen island. A spread of eggs, bacon, sausage, fresh fruit and pastries spanned the entire length of the marble countertop. Her eyes sparkled, mulling over what to choose first.

****

Bayfield strolled into the kitchen moments later, his gaze skimming the crowd for Arielle. As he caught sight of her, he stood motionless, staring. Her long dark hair shimmered beneath the pendant lighting, and a clingy T-shirt and skintight jeans embraced her body. His heart pummeled inside his chest as he sailed across the room to reach her.

"Good morning," he breathed, resting his hand on the small of her back.

"Good morning," she echoed, her stomach fluttering, set off by his voice, his touch. She faced him, savoring every inch of his biceps and muscular torso clothed in a fitted black T-shirt. The front of the shirt, he tucked into a pair of faded black Levi's. Peeking out from underneath his jeans were the coolest Doc Martens ever! Her jaw dropped a smidgen as her brain conjured up his taste—*trendy*. She locked her eyes on his, a glowing expression capturing her face before she snapped out of the enchantment. "Wow, you got here fast. I was expecting to eat alone. How was the workout?"

He offered her a wink. "My workout was at 6 a.m., and it was great, thanks. Was just getting out of the shower when you slipped the note under my door." He glanced down at her T-shirt. "Ya know, I make a killer Latte."

"Really? Can you make a heart in the foam?"

"Yep."

"Let's grab some breakfast, then you can show me your coffee skills."

"You got it."

They rounded the island and worked the buffet by stacking eggs, bacon, and fruit onto their plates. Bayfield spotted a vacant table just shy of one of the many windows and snagged it. He rubbed his hands together. "Get ready to witness perfection."

Arielle huffed. "Perfection? Come on."

He took her hand, leading her toward the coffee bar. "I'm serious. You'll see."

She perched a hand on her hip as she stood back to behold his version of perfection. "Let's see what you've got."

He packed the espresso before sliding it into the machine. As the rich roast ran into the cup, he steamed the milk, tipping the pitcher as the machine whirled to life. With a look of concentration, he let the milk flow, dragging it through the dark coffee, creating a beautiful white heart. With a proud grin, he handed her his masterpiece.

She glanced into the cup, then at him. "You weren't kidding. This is stunning. I almost don't want to drink it."

He shrugged as he began fixing a cup for himself. "My first job was at Old-Fashioned Coffee."

"Ooh, love the name." She took a sip and her eyes rolled back in her head. "Oh my God, delish!"

He gave her a playful nudge. "Told ya."

Taking another sip, she batted her eyelashes at him. "Mmm."

A beaming smile lit up his face. "After we finish breakfast, I'll make you another one."

She gave him a curt nod. "Deal."

With coffees in hand, they strolled back to their table, seduced by the perks of Drara's palace. Bayfield pulled out Arielle's chair, and an inner glow danced inside her eyes. He possessed such thoughtful, sincere attributes, unlike any guy she'd ever met, and she'd met her fair share of losers only after looks and money. Bayfield had noticed her looks, sure, but he didn't seem to give a crap about money, not even a little bit. Her heart purred at the thought, signaling its approval of him.

He stabbed a forkful of fluffy eggs, then focused his attention on her. "How do you feel about checking out the library and taking the books to the garden to read?"

She couldn't contain her smile. "Oh, I'd love that. You think of..." Her voice faded to a whisper.

Bayfield watched her pupils dilate, fixated on something over his shoulder. "What's is it? What's wrong?" He didn't wait for a reply as he twisted in his chair. His vision fell upon a petite woman slumped in a wheelchair, her reddish-brown hair spouting flecks of gray at her temples. A stocky set man navigated her to a spot drenched in sunlight before setting the brake and mumbling something to her. Not a trace of acknowledgment flickered in her distant stare as he walked away. Bayfield's gaze darted back to Arielle. "Her scenario doesn't fit."

Arielle pushed her food around her plate, shaking her head. "She shouldn't be here."

"Peeps!" Tommy's voice bellowed throughout the kitchen. Clad in striped surfer shorts, a light blue T-shirt, and his customary flip-flops, he approached Bayfield and Arielle. "Breakfast was awesome today. Am I right, or am I right?"

Arielle's eyes darted to the woman. "She couldn't possibly have signed Drara's book," she surmised to Tommy. "No way. It's not physically or mentally possible. Forget comprehension, what about the state she's in? No one would want to stay trapped like that. She can't even defend herself. Why is she here? What happened?"

Tommy blew an impatient snort. "Take a breath, Kojak."

She scrunched her brows together. "What?"

Bayfield grimaced. "Who the hell is Kojak?"

"He's a TV—" Tommy waved Bayfield away. "It doesn't matter. Listen, things are different here. They don't always make sense."

Bayfield stood and crossed his arms. "What aren't you telling us?"

Tommy held his hands up. "Hey, I don't make the rules, and the truth is, we don't know what happened to Sara."

Arielle got to her feet. "Is that her name, Sara?" Tommy nodded. "So she wasn't like that when she arrived?" Arielle pressed.

"No," Tommy explained. "She was like everyone else. One day she was fine, the next she wasn't."

"I'm gonna go talk to her." Arielle didn't wait for a reply and started toward the woman.

"She can't talk," Tommy called after her.

Bayfield tilted his body toward Tommy and pointed out, "We'll see." He shoved his hands in his pockets and shadowed Arielle.

Tommy groaned before trundling after them.

Arielle knelt before the woman. "Hi, Sara. My name's Arielle," she said, her tone gentle. "I wanted to meet you."

The woman's gaze remained focused out the window. Something in the distance seemed to draw her eye.

Arielle squinted, searching the grounds for the object capturing the woman's attention. Beautiful trees with red and orange leaves filled her vision. "Do you want to go outside?" Arielle asked.

The woman's gaze darted to hers and locked there.

Arielle glanced up at Bayfield. "I think she wants to go outside?"

Tommy waved his hands back and forth. "Bad idea."

"You said we could leave anytime," Bayfield challenged. "If she wants to go outside, so what?"

Tommy forced a laugh. "Just because she gave Arielle bug eyes, doesn't mean she wants to leave the house. You two are reading too much into it." He wagged a finger at them. "Like I said, it hurts like a son of a bitch. I'm sure she doesn't want to go through that."

Arielle lobbed a hard squint at Tommy, then faced Sara, offering her a pleasant smile. "Sara, do you want us to take you outside?"

Sara's glare strengthened, her whites showing.

"Not good enough," Tommy argued.

Arielle rested a hand on Sara's knee. "Sara, if you want to go outside, blink once for yes and twice for no."

The veins in Sara's neck bulged as the flesh around her face grew taut. Her eyelashes struggled into a single blink."

"Ha!" Bayfield shouted. "There, you see? She does."

Arielle patted Sara's knee, then rose and crossed her arms. "We're taking her outside."

"I don't know, man." Tommy paused and cleared his throat. "Seems pretty risky."

"How risky can it be?" Bayfield questioned before he flashed a sly wink toward Arielle. "Besides, Arielle and I are taking a trip to the hospital today to check on our progress. We can take Sara with us."

"That's right," Arielle confirmed. "It's no trouble bringing her along."

Tommy's gaze bounced back and forth between them as he pursed his lips. "I was trying to save you the pain, but you know what they say, that actions speak louder than words. Go for it. Take her with you. It'll hurt like hell, and then you'll know."

Arielle didn't hesitate to grab Sara's wheelchair and scurry away.

"We'll take good care of Sara," Bayfield assured before jogging after them.

Tommy waved them away, mumbling, "They're gonna wish they'd listened to me."

Chapter 9

Bayfield cracked the front door open and peeked out. Beams of sunlight danced across the massive archway as a warm breeze scattered leaves toward the doorway. He pushed the door wide open and inched a foot past the threshold. Bayfield was no stranger to pain. He'd been knocked around the ring plenty of times, but this was different. This whole thing was foreign to him, and he had Arielle and Sara to look out for. He straddled the doorway—one leg in, one leg out.

Arielle paced Sara's wheelchair back and forth just inside the doorway, her hands clenched about the handles. "Do you feel anything?" Her soft voice bore an edge to it.

Bayfield showed his palms and shrugged. "No, nothing." He slowly slid all the way out and rooted his feet to the stone pavement. Still nothing. Where was this massive pain Tommy had preached about? Maybe Tommy was full of it. Whatever the case, he stood free of pain. He waved Arielle out, and she parked Sara's wheelchair next to Bayfield, rubbing the blood back into her white knuckles. Had she been gripping the handles that hard?

Bayfield left her side and swung the front door closed. As it settled into its frame, a series of tiny blasts echoed in his ears. "Did you hear—" An unhuman force invaded his body, slamming it against the ground. The impact scraped off layers of flesh, smarting down to the exposed bone. Bayfield belted out a guttural scream, yet the torture persisted. The powerful suction ripped the imposter's shell off his soul, shredding muscle and breaking bones. He convulsed into a fetal position, eyes glazed over, breaths shallow, drifting in and out of consciousness.

The shrill pitch of Arielle's screams pierced Bayfield's brain, pushing him to his feet. His legs wobbled, threating to collapse as he staggered toward her. With every step, that weird and wonderful lightness of his human soul flooded back, dominating over the demise of his imposter body.

He scooped Arielle's crumpled body off the ground and cupped her face in his hands. Over her cries, he shouted, "Arielle, look at me!"

The wounded look in her eyes landed on his face. Recognition flashed, causing a torrent of tears to stream down her cheeks. She hugged her quaking body and struggled to speak. "I f–feel like I–I'm on f–fire."

He pulled her into his embrace and smoothed her hair. "It'll be over soon. I promise."

She sank against him, letting out a huge breath. The burning sting weakened, inching down her arms and legs before freeing her. Arielle pressed her palms into her eyes, wiping away tears.

Bayfield held her at arm's length, his eyes searching hers, spotting that copper gleam. "Better?"

"Yes," she sighed.

Sara's wheelchair thumped against the pavement, turning both Arielle's and Bayfield's heads. Her whole body convulsed as slimy goo drooled out of the corner of her mouth.

"Sara!" Arielle cried.

Bayfield knelt at Sara's side. "Sara, can you hear me?"

Sara flopped back and forth in the chair, gagging out more goo.

Bayfield glanced at Arielle. "I think she's choking on something." He peered inside her mouth and caught the end of a black tentacle slithering across her tongue. "Jesus," Bayfield blurted out, shuffling back a step.

Arielle lunged toward Sara. "What? What is it?"

Bayfield blocked her with his arm. "Stay back."

White foam bubbled over Sara's lips as her violent retching spewed out a slimy black centipede about the size of a rat.

Arielle shrieked and tumbled back, hitting the ground. Springing upright like a cat, she balled her fists, ready to fight.

Bayfield raised his foot, aiming it over the creature. Before his shoe made contact, the monstrous centipede shattered into a million pieces and vanished into the air. "Holy shit."

"Oh my God!" Arielle cried. "What the hell was that?"

"No fucking clue."

Sara jumped to her feet, freeing a pent-up scream and driving a foot into the wheelchair. As if to mock her, the chair endured its stationary position. Again, she shoved a heel into its side without budging it an inch. Her fists pummeled the leather seat, but the chair showed no remorse, not even a shudder of reaction. Sara hunched over, letting her hands go limp as a vacant stare claimed her. She collapsed in front of the chair, sobbing into her hands.

Arielle knelt beside her to offer a comforting touch, yet her hand slipped right through Sara's shoulder. Arielle flinched and scrambled to her feet, reaching for Bayfield. As his fingers slipped between hers, Arielle let out a gasp, her gaze darting to Sara. "What are you? Why can't I touch you? And what the hell came out of you?"

Sara stared into her palms, shaking her head and answering in a muted voice, "For five years, I sat mute in that chair." She shot daggers at the wheelchair. "No one noticed my suffering." She glanced at Arielle and Bayfield. "Until you. And I'm human, just like you."

Bayfield locked his arms in a confrontational stance and bobbed his chin toward Sara. "If you're human, why'd Arielle's hand sink inside you? And no human I know has creepy crawlers living inside of them."

Sara slowly pushed to her feet, a tragic smile spreading across her lips. "It's easier if I just show you, but you'll have to come with me."

Bayfield flattened his lips and gave a firm shake of his head. "Hell no. Not after what I just saw. You have to give us something we can believe before we up and follow you to who knows where."

"What he said," Arielle affirmed.

Sara eyed them a good while before offering up an explanation. "Living matter connects our soul to its body. The body dies, the connection is broken."

"Are you saying..." Arielle covered her mouth and looked away.

Bayfield wrapped an arm around Arielle's shoulders, yet his eyes never left Sara's.

"I died. That's why you can't touch me," Sara confirmed. "A lonely soul is what I've become, and before I share more, I'd really like to get the hell away from this place."

Bayfield wasn't buying it. "Maybe you died, maybe you didn't. For all we know, you could be one of those freaks,"—he bobbed his head toward the mansion—"who's lost touch with reality."

Arielle focused her attention on Sara. Her dull eyes lacked that hint of copper Arielle and Jonathan carried. "Jonathan, look at her eyes. The light inside them is gone...like, really gone. I believe her. I think she's telling the truth."

He squinted, recognizing the void in Sara's eyes, but he wasn't ready to fold just yet. "There's still a lot of unanswered questions."

"And I'll explain, but not here."

"Just one problem," Bayfield pointed out. "Invisible people don't drive, so how do we get to where it is you want us to go?"

A knowing grin brightened Sara's face. "I can take us there."

"But—"

Sara didn't let Arielle finish. "It's true, you can't touch me, yet *I* can lay hands on you and transport us to the location." She leaned in and lowered her voice. "Let me fill you in on a little secret. Energy connects our soul to its frame. Merely concentrating on it will transport your soul to its body. However, the energy doesn't work in reverse. Coming back to Drara's can be rather tricky."

"Then how do we get back?"

"City transportation. Buses are always running, but as you indicated, we can't be seen. The bus isn't going to stop for obscured souls." She shrugged. "Finding people getting on and off where you need to go is the tricky part."

"Seems pretty iffy." Bayfield looked to Arielle. "You wanna chance it? You in?"

Arielle gave a slight nod. "I want to hear what she has to say. I'm in."

"We're in."

"Here we go," Sara said, laying her hands on them.

Arielle's eyelashes fluttered, as if trapped inside a dream, before springing wide open. A grassy hill stretched out in front her, dotted with graves. Bayfield stood on her right and Sara her left, a cluster of pine trees towering above them. An ache swelled in Arielle's throat as her gaze traveled over the marker at her feet: *Sara Clark, Beloved Wife and Mother. So dearly loved, so sadly missed.* Arielle's eyes darted to Sara. "The magic...the book... How could this happen?"

Bayfield draped a comforting arm around Arielle's shoulders, shifting his focus to Sara. "I can't imagine what you must be feeling. This is shitty and selfish, but I have to know what happened."

Sara's spine bowed and her shoulders quaked. "Drara's..." She struggled to control her voice, then summoned an inner strength she'd harvested over the past five years. "Drara's magic did not keep its promise. On one of my many trips to the hospital, I happened upon an upheaval of nurses and doctors rushing about my room. My husband and daughter huddled in the corner, sobbing, as the medical staff pummeled my chest and forced air into my lungs. I remembered thinking *this can't be,* and then that horrible, unmistakable sound hit. The monitor flatlined, and the words *time of death* slammed against my eardrums. My mind went numb, I blinked, and then there was Drara's yellowish orbs gazing at me."

An image of creepy Catwoman flashed behind Arielle's eyes, launching a cold shudder across her spine. Fleeing in the opposite direction spun about her brain, but learning the truth kept her feet rooted to the ground. Bayfield picked up on the section 8 vibes bouncing off of Arielle and wrapped both of his arms around her, holding her tight. She peered up at him, eyes sparkling, her phobia alarm bells growing faint.

A satisfied sigh escaped Sara as she gazed at the young couple. At least they had the comfort of each other trapped inside Drara's nightmare, yet the inability for that happily-ever-after was not in their favor, and heightened her urgency to divulge all she knew.

"I confronted Drara, reminding her she'd promised my soul would have a body to return to, that I'd signed her book, gave her my blood to prevent my death." Sara's gaze clouded over as she recalled her body, pale and void of life, stretched out on the hospital bed. Forcing out a labored breath, she shunned the past and resumed her tale. "Drara showed zero emotion, not even a flutter of an eyelash. I'd thrusted a finger toward my body, screaming at the top of my lungs for her to fix it. She'd peered at me with those cat-like eyes and said, "Of course." She reached for my hand and folded my fingers around something that resembled a red kidney bean. I remember her voice rang with authority as she told me to go back to her palace. Once inside, and only then, I was to swallow the bean whole."

"And you trusted her?" Arielle threw at Sara.

"Arielle!" Bayfield scolded. "Show some compassion."

"No, it's okay, really," Sara assured. "And Arielle's right. I shouldn't have trusted Drara." Sara stepped into Arielle's personal space and locked eyes with her. "But I was desperate, my mind on my grieving husband and daughter. I wasn't ready to leave them."

Arielle reached out to touch Sara, and then pulled away. "I'm such an ass. I have this nasty habit of just blurting shit out. I'm sorry. Of course you weren't ready."

"Thank you." Sara pursed her lips. "I did as Drara instructed. Her monstrous bean crippled me, left me mute. For five years, I sat trapped, pleading with my eyes for someone in the damned palace to feel my pain. I'd lived there with those fools for two years prior to my death, and not one of them asked what happened, how I ended up in a wheel-chair, unable to speak. They just looked the other way." Her eyes found Arielle's. "Until you. You noticed, and you freed me from my torment."

"In my mind, there wasn't a question in what you wanted," Arielle admitted with a nod. "They're all cowards for not helping you."

"Maybe," Sara offered.

"So you knew the outside world would destroy the creature," Bayfield speculated.

Sara shrugged. "Every time any of us walked out that door, her magic disintegrated. I'd hoped it would have the same effect on the thing I'd swallowed."

"Well, thank God it did," Arielle said. "To be stuck like that for five years? I can't even imagine." Arielle tilted her head to the side. "So, like, why hasn't your soul, ya know, moved on?"

Bayfield scolded, "There you go again, just blurting shit out."

Arielle offered him a half-hearted shrug.

Sara looked thoughtful as she pondered Arielle's words. "That's a good question. Unfortunately, I don't have the answer. If I had to make an educated guess, I'd say it has something to do with Drara's book."

"We could work together," Bayfield suggested.

Sara leaned forward. "How so?"

Bayfield's gaze bounced between Arielle and Sara as he rattled off, "Seems like Drara's got a hidden agenda, and we're all pieces in her chess game. Obviously, Sara can't go back to the house, but with Sara on the outside, and Arielle and I on the inside, maybe we can uncover details about Drara and her mysterious book."

"Are you insane? Do you want some creepy bug crammed down your throat? Snooping around is too dangerous. What if we get caught?" Arielle grabbed Bayfield's arm. "We can't go back either. We show up without Sara, everyone's gonna be suspicious, and Catwoman might have moles on the inside."

Bayfield stroked her back, nodding. "You might be right."

"I am right."

"What if you say I flipped out," Sara suggested. "Started ranting crazy stuff and ran off."

"How would we even exchange information?" Bayfield questioned, still considering the idea.

"We'd need to agree on a time and location to meet," Sara replied.

"If I go back to the house, I'm not leaving it." Arielle shuddered away a chill and hugged her arms. "I can't go through that pain again. It felt like I was being ripped apart and set on fire."

"It was crazy intense," Bayfield echoed. "Wouldn't want to go through that hell again." He had an obligation to safeguard Arielle. If she wasn't going back, then neither was he. "I won't leave you alone out here. Whatever you decide, I'm with you, one hundred percent."

Arielle's eyes grew glassy as her hand fluttered over her heart. "I've never met anyone like you, ever." She rose onto her tiptoes and kissed him as though she'd never take another breath.

Bayfield cradled her head in his hands, stroking her hair and kissing her, aware of his own heartbeat confessing his feelings for her.

"This is sweet, but we need to come to a decision. Are you going back to Drara's, or staying on the outside with me?"

Bayfield looked to Arielle.

She grabbed his hand. "I can't go back."

Bayfield squeezed hers before turning to Sara. "The outside it is."

Chapter 10

Jekins settled into his favorite wingback chair, took a sip of Earl Grey tea, and stretched his legs toward the fireplace. A hint of citrus delighted his senses as the crackling flames danced inside the hearth. He sank deeper into the worn cushions, his eyelids sliding closed.

"Why have you not answered me?" Drara's voice interrupted the peaceful silence. "I will not tolerate being ignored."

Jekins kept his eyes closed as he responded with, "Hello, Drara. I don't think you've grasped the concept of knocking, and then waiting to be invited into someone's home. Furthermore, I haven't ignored you. We set boundaries, remember? I provide my services up until 7 p.m. The remainder of the night belongs to me. Whomever has relinquished their soul and autographed your book can wait until tomorrow morning."

An impatient huff vibrated in his right ear before she countered with, "I made no such agreement."

Jekins twisted in his chair to face her. "You may not have expressed your agreement verbally; however, my terms stand firm." He rose to his feet and towered over her. "I'm not a young man anymore, Drara. I need to rest my bones before I trudge about the earth and gather your wayward souls."

"I pay you handsomely for your services. You want for nothing."

"This is true."

Her voice reeked with authority. "Therefore, when I request your services, you must be available."

He matched her tone. "During the hours I stated."

"Don't test me, Jekins."

"Or what, Drara? You need me. Besides, you're not the type."

Her yellowish orbs constricted as she stood completely still. "The type to what? You are aware of my power, and I have grown fond of you. I would hate to have to find another human."

He took a sip of tea and waved her away. "Threaten much, Drara?"

A black vein bulged in the center of her translucent forehead. She took a single step, clenching her hands.

"All right, all right. Relax," Jekins conceded. "I will collect your souls, but in the morning." He smirked. "It's not like they're going anywhere." He pointed to a second chair facing the fireplace. "Take a load off, Drara, and have some tea."

"I do not require tea."

"Well, then, have a seat. Enjoy the fire."

Drara fingered the skeleton key dangling around her neck as she lowered herself into the chair. She sat perfectly straight, her hands resting on her knees, her eyes focused on the hearth. As she cocked her head and squinted at the blaze, her gray braids fell to one side. The orange and yellow flames crackling about the burnt wood stirred memories of her creation. Images shuffled across the surface of her brain before falling into place.

A hollow skeleton had arisen from a flash of light, its frame thrown inside of a spinning abyss of magic. The skeleton morphed into solid shapes: a head, torso, limbs. The rotation accelerated, shifting the pieces into a feminine form as liquid metal had cascaded over translucent flesh and hardening into protective armor. A female figure emerged and had held herself erect, conscious of her purpose—to govern human souls.

Drara blinked, the present flooding back, her gaze landing on the black veins etched into her skin. A slight growl swelled in her throat as she cursed the magic that made her. Humans did not look this way. Their pale pinkish flesh possessed the beauty of angels.

"Do you see me as hideous?"

Jekins's eyes widened at the creature he'd served for forty years. "No, of course not."

She looked down at her body. "I do not know why I was made to look as I do."

He leaned forward in his chair, narrowing the gap between them. "Who wants to look like everyone else?"

An empty stare filled her yellowish orbs. "I do."

Jekins placed his hand over hers. "Drara, there's nothing wrong with the way you look."

"There is," she disagreed. "My appearance frightens people."

He pointed to himself. "I'm a person. I'm not frightened."

"Because you are my human."

"Because I'm open-minded." He waved her away. "Besides, being human is overrated. It's a hard life, Drara, with lots of ups and downs, something you should think twice about."

She smirked. "You cannot sway me, Jekins. I will become human."

Chapter 11

Coach stepped inside the elevator and punched the button for the ICU floor, shifting the backpack of mementos from home to his left shoulder. He'd never married, never wanted kids. Boxing was his life. He'd come out of his mother's womb swinging and never stopped, and by no means inside the ring either. He had a knack for managing, recognizing talent, and producing stars and champions. Trophies lined the walls of his boxing club, but fulfilling dreams was his true reward.

Eons ago, his two best friends, Mack and Janis, had asked him to be Jonathan's only godparent. Friends since college, he felt he had to do right by them. He was just a fill-in for date nights mostly, and family type stuff. He'd never dreamed he'd end up as dad materiel, yet there he was, ten years later, a father figure to Jonathan. Being a parent had come with many challenges, but he'd loved that kid more than his own life. Tears pricked his eyes, but it wasn't the time to fall apart. Jonathan needed his strength now more than ever. Coach toughened up, sucking in a few quick breaths, tossing the emotions on the back burner.

The chime of the elevator announced its arrival to the ICU. Coach breezed down the hall, veering toward Jonathan's room, a nervous flutter brushing the walls of his stomach. An article he'd read last night, *Coma Simulation,* seemed promising. It kicked around the importance of regular visits—yet not to overstimulate. The patient needed their own quiet time. Physical contact, placing objects in their hands, wiping their face with a soft cloth, the article suggested as highly successful simulants, as well as showing family photos, talking about familiarities, and playing their favorite music.

Steps from Jonathan's room, Coach let the backpack slide off his shoulder, the contents jangling in protest. Over the clanks, he recognized Dr. Yoo's soft-spoken voice. As he entered, he found the doctor standing at the foot of Jonathan's bed, skimming through his electronic chart and rattling off numbers to a nurse on his right.

Coach set the pack on the floor and barged right into the middle of their conversation. "How's Jonathan today? Any change?"

Dr. Yoo acknowledged Coach with a nod, then returned his gaze to the chart. "The EEG shows the abnormal brain activity is decreasing. Some of the swelling has subsided as well."

"That's good, right?"

"Yes..."

Coach inhaled a breath and blew it out quickly. "Sounds like there was a "but" in there somewhere."

Dr. Yoo's smooth brow furrowed. "With these numbers, he should be waking up. I'm puzzled as to why he hasn't."

Coach scooped up his backpack and gave it a pat. "I've got just the trick right here, Dr. Yoo." He yanked on the zipper, giving the doctor a peek of its contents. "Trophies, photos, clothes, and music. All familiar things to Jonathan."

"Very good, Mr. Meyers. I'm sure these items will help."

Coach positioned each piece randomly about the narrow room, but Jonathan's very first trophy from high school, he set inside Jonathan's palm. The hum of the ventilator overshadowed Coach's thoughts. He glared at the machine briefly before calling out and stopping Dr. Yoo at the door.

"Dr. Yoo, any chance Jonathan can come off this thing soon?"

Dr. Yoo gave him an understanding nod. "The healing process is a slow process, Mr. Meyers. Let's take it one day at a time."

Coach tapped his fingers against his leg, releasing the negative energy. "Good plan."

"Enjoy your visit."

"Thank you."

Coach sat next to Jonathan and squeezed his hand around the trophy. "Ya gotta give them something, buddy. Ya gotta show them you're still in there." He snatched up the backpack and waved an MP3 player in front of Jonathan. "Downloaded our faves from Guns N' Roses on this bad boy. Ya ready?" Coach pressed play and grooved to "Sweet Child O' Mine."

Chapter 12

Arielle, Sara, and Bayfield camped out in a discarded rundown church marked for demolition. The trio transformed the frayed floorboards into a parade of reference books, newspaper clippings, and articles, yet not one mentioned the mysterious Drara.

Arielle snapped another book closed, sprinkling the air with dust. "What we need is one of those Indiana Jones types."

Bayfield gave Arielle a playful nudge. "Cute."

Sara considered the suggestion. "She might have something there."

Bayfield rolled his eyes. "Oh, come on."

Sara grabbed one of the many books littering the floor and waved it in front of him. "Hear me out. What if we located an archaeologist, one who favors the bizarre? We need someone who understands the nature of the book and a creature like Drara, who can easily track down information. Someone who has access to multiple research databases. I've got a professor friend. He might be of some help digging up said archaeologist." She chuckled. "No pun intended."

Arielle gave a thumbs-up. "I like it."

Bayfield heaved a sigh. "Your friend isn't gonna shoot the shit with someone he can't see."

Sara slapped Bayfield on the back. "O ye, of little faith. My friend just also happens to be of the psychic persuasion. If Jekins can see us, so can Randall."

Arielle tucked her arm inside Bayfield's. "It's worth a try. I mean, it's not like we've got tons of options."

Bayfield surrendered. "Why the hell not?"

"You two should stay in body range, it's safer. And since mine, well, ya know...died, I'll go alone and try to get Randall to come here. There's a snowball's chance in hell of this working out, so don't get your hopes up."

"Now that, I'm in agreement with," Bayfield confirmed.

Arielle shrugged away the skepticism. "Too late. Full-on optimistic here."

Bayfield wrapped an arm around Arielle, the girl he'd leaned on during this nightmare. He'd fallen in love with her soul, even before he could touch her human body. If that wasn't true love, then he didn't know what was. "He'll come," he assured, then bobbed his chin toward Sara. "So, what's your plan?"

"I'm getting fairly good at using my soul energy to travel. I'll pop over to the university and track Randall down." Sara spread her arms wide, palms up. "We'll see if he freaks. If he does, we're out of luck and back to square one. If he's cool with the weirdness of it all, I'll lay out the facts of this debacle and bring him back here, hopefully with an archaeologist or some type of researcher who *can* help us."

Bayfield nudged Arielle's shoulder. "While Sara's putting feelers out on Randall, we could do a hospital run and check on our progress."

Arielle drew her mouth into a straight line. The hospital didn't give her the warm and fuzzies as it did Jonathan, but he had Coach. Her parents were MIA, which was just more validation that she didn't matter. But for him, Arielle conjured up a convincing smile. "Absolutely. Let's do it."

****

Randall was a creature of habit, so Sara knew exactly where to find him. She snuck into his office and stood in the background, shaking her head and thinking how some things never changed. He sat hunched over his desk, chewing on a toothpick, glasses low on his nose as he graded papers to the burning glow of a single lamp. His mop of hair, still a wild mess of curls, fell into his eyes. Sara flipped on the overhead light, brightening the dimly lit room and announcing her presence. "Hello, Randall."

Randall spit out the toothpick and ejected out of his chair. "Jesus, Sara." His eyes widened, and then narrowed as her circumstances registered inside his psychic brain. "What the hell happened to you?"

Sara glided closer, a grave expression pulling her face taut. "I died."

He cupped a hand over his mouth. "God, I'm so sorry." His brow furrowed as he pointed out, "But me being able to see you means that whatever tragedy has befallen you is also not allowing you to move on."

"I'm afraid so," she admitted. "I need your help."

"Help? With what, you moving on? I'm not sure I've got any experience with something like that."

Sara nodded. "Yes, I want to move on." Her voice cracked and she closed her eyes, blowing out a few calming breaths before continuing. "But that's not why I'm here. I need information. You see, I'm looking for answers about a book."

"A book?" He laughed nervously. "Seems rather pointless at this stage of the game, don't you think?"

Sara gave him a serious look. "Well, not really. I'm certain this book is the reason why I can't move on. It's what's keeping me earthbound."

"How so?"

"It's a long story." She waved off the details. "I'll give you the CliffsNotes version. An accident put me in a coma. I'd had one of those out-of-body experiences, and was presented with a book which if signed, would keep me alive." She tapped her right temple. "You can't image what goes through your mind when you're standing over your own body, so I didn't hesitate to sign." She gestured to herself. "But as you can see, the book didn't hold up its end of the bargain. I died, and somehow, I'm still linked to this book. Or, I should say, my soul is. I have to find a way to free myself from it."

Randall held up his hands, splaying his fingers. "Whoa, wait a minute. You're talking about a mystical book?"

She stared him down, attempting to read him, yet she hit a solid wall. "I don't know the origin of this book, but with everything I've seen, my guess is that it's quite sinister, and it's stopping me from moving on."

An unfocused gaze claimed his eyes as he opened his mouth, yet he offered no reply.

"There's one more thing." Sara swallowed hard. Exposing Drara would probably push him over the edge, but there wasn't a choice. Drara and the book were a package deal. In one breath, she forced out the rest. "A creature possesses this book."

"Creature?" He said the word out loud to substantiate he'd heard her right. "This is way out there, Sara. I may be psychic, but this sounds…"

Sara clenched her fists and let loose her frustration with a loud groan. "I know how it sounds, Randall. I'm the one trapped in the middle of this freakish nightmare."

He shook his head. "Why come to me? I don't know what I can do."

She clasped her hands in a pleading fashion. "Please, come with me to talk to the others. I'm not the only one who signed, and unlike me, the others are still alive. Help us gather information on the book."

He slumped into his chair, his thoughts scrambling to understand. "Man, Sara, this is way outside of my wheelhouse."

"We're invisible, Randall," she put before him in the shrillest tone. "You being psychic helps us immensely. You can talk with people, travel, gain information where we can't."

"You're talking out of body experiences, souls that can't move on, mystical books, creatures!" He stumbled over his words. "That's… that's…I can't even." He looked directly at her. "No, Sara, I'm truly sorry. I can't help you. I wouldn't know where to begin."

Randall wasn't going to budge. Her shoulders slumped as she nodded. "I understand. At the very least, do you know of anyone who *can* help us?"

"Rue Cohen," he rattled off, wanting to rid himself of Sara and her book. "One crazy-ass archaeologist. She gets off on that shit. Got a warehouse full of unearthly relics." He flipped through his phone, then scribbled down her number. "Here's her cell. Problem is, she's in India on an excavation, but I'd be willing to bet she'll get her ass on a plane as soon as she hears about that book."

****

Bayfield and Arielle made it to the hospital after hopping on several buses and trekking a good half mile. Arielle hung back, determined to make the best of the situation, and to do that, she put her own room on hold and tagged along with Bayfield. As they strode into his room, the world of eighties rock greeted them. Bayfield froze, his chin dipping toward his chest. "Oh my God, he's playing Guns N' Roses."

Arielle whipped her head back and forth, imitating a head banger rockin' out. "Partay!"

"Very funny."

She smoothed her hair back in place, then lightly touched his arm. "I think it's sweet." She pointed at Coach. "He's reading something to you."

As Bayfield pulled Coach into a bear hug, his gaze landed on the newspaper. "An article on my first boxing match. I was the breakout star." Bayfield released Coach, sniffling and swiping his eyes.

Arielle hugged Bayfield as tight as she could. "We're gonna get through this."

He kissed the top of her head, then gave her a faint smile.

The trophies scattered across the room caught her eye. "What a trip. Look at all these. You were quite the athlete, yeah?"

A proud expression took over his face. "I was indeed."

Picture frames adorned the room. One of a kid with a goofy grin sat beside the hospital bed, facing his body. Arielle cupped a hand over her mouth, smothering her laughter. "Is that you?"

"Yes," he groaned, then glared at Coach. "My sixth-grade pic? Why, Coach, why?"

Arielle's gaze darted about, taking in each photo. "This is so wonderful, Jonathan."

"Yeah," Bayfield admitted, his focus lingering on Coach before shifting to the machines and tubes. "Doesn't look like my condition has changed much."

"But you're still alive. That's what matters."

He laughed. "Thank God." His eyes met hers. "You want me to go with you to your room?"

Knowing her room wasn't going to be anything like his, Arielle reached for his hand. "I'd like that." Arielle led him down the hall and toward room 410. Inches from the doorway, a shudder ran through her.

What if she'd died? Sara's theory of body and soul connection squashed that thought. And Jonathan's hand wrapped around hers ensured her that her body hadn't died.

"You okay?"

"I can't look. Will you look for me and tell me what you see?"

"Of course." Bayfield popped his head inside the doorway, then glanced back at Arielle. "There's a man and a woman with you."

"What?" Arielle dashed past him, her eyes landing on her mother and father huddled about her bed, each holding her hands. She skidded to a stop, her mouth falling open, releasing a strangled sob.

Bayfield rushed to her, taking her hand. "What is it? What's wrong?"

"My... My parents are here."

"That's good, right?"

She'd never seen her mother with wet dull eyes, or her father bowed over like an old man. Who were these people, and what had they done with her self-centered parents? Arielle's expression crumpled as she said, "I...I don't know."

Bayfield stroked her back, attempting to comfort her. "It's gonna be okay."

Her vision blurred. She couldn't wipe the tears away fast enough, and more continued to fall, the relentless sobs dominating very breath. "I h–have to g–get out of h–here."

Bayfield whisked her away, ushering her to safety inside a quiet room down the hall. She shook uncontrollably in his arms. "Shh, it's okay. I'm here for you."

Arielle sagged against him, using his strength to heal her bruised heart. "All I ever wanted was for them to love me. I never got that, ever." Her voice weakened. "My whole life, I was alone. They were never around." She jutted a hand in the direction of her room. "*Now* they de-cide to show up!"

Bayfield offered an understanding nod. "I'm only an outsider looking in, but what I saw was two grieving and devastated parents. Sometimes people take others for granted. They're probably clinging to the hope that you'll survive so they can right their wrongs."

"Maybe." Her tone was uncertain.

"Why don't we go back into your room and you can judge for yourself?"

A pained expression came over her. "I don't know if I can."

"I'll be with you."

Taking a deep breath, she attempted to gain control over her emotions. "Okay."

He joined their hands and slowly led her back to her room. Her parents hadn't moved, still glued to her bedside and gripping her hands. Bayfield nudged her toward the foot of her bed.

"Arielle," Denise said, yet no other words formed. Her mother swiped at her eyes and looked to her husband.

Carey cleared his throat several times, his voice still raspy when he finally spoke. "Honey, we're here. We won't leave your side, we promise."

Her mother squeezed Arielle's hand, nodding.

Carey kissed Arielle's forehead and whispered, "You're strong, baby. You fight this."

Arielle rested her hand on her father's shoulder. "I'm fighting, Dad, more than you know."

Chapter 13

Sara strutted toward Bayfield and Arielle as they stepped inside the church, a confident smile settled on her lips.

Bayfield stopped in his tracks. "Jesus, you're already back? That can't be good."

Arielle said nothing as she slumped into one of the pews, resting her head in her hands.

Sara bobbed her chin in Arielle's direction. "What gives?"

"Emotional day. Her parents were at the hospital."

"Ah." Sara nodded, as if Arielle's past was secondhand knowledge.

Bayfield skimmed the church. "No Randall? Are we back to square one?"

Sara paused, letting the anticipation build before rattling off, "Randall freaked, wanting nothing to do with our cause. But he did give me some info and a name, probably just to get rid of me."

"An archaeologist?"

"Yes. And not just any old archaeologist." Sara glanced at Arielle and raised her voice. "An *Indiana Jones* type."

Arielle quickly perked up. "Really?"

"Yep. Now get your ass over here so I don't have to say this twice."

Arielle rose and dragged herself to where the two were standing together.

Sara waited, ensuring she had their undivided attention. "The archaeologist's name is Rue Cohen. Randall says the government funds her excavations, and most are for bizarre, unexplainable artifacts. Downside is, she's currently in India."

"India?" Bayfield rolled his eyes. "How's that good news?"

Sara sighed. "It's a lead."

Arielle threw up her hands. "Not if we can't get to her."

Sara wagged her finger at the skeptics. "We're not going to talk to her. We're gonna get Jekins to."

Arielle huffed, waving a dismissive hand toward Sara.

Bayfield laughed. "No offense, but I think that thing Drara put inside you killed off some of your brain cells. There's no way her right-hand man is going to betray her."

"How can you be certain?" Sara snatched up a book and waved it at them. "We don't know anything about the guy or what he thinks. Maybe he'll have a conscience."

"Well, look what the cat dragged in," a male voice interrupted.

The three whipped their heads toward the voice, finding a tall, lean figure standing inside the doorway, the sun's rays streaming behind him and blocking his appearance.

Bayfield squinted, trying to make him out. "You can see us?"

As the man closed the door, his pitch-black hair slicked back into a ponytail and benevolent expression came into view. "Of course I can. You're standing in the middle of my church."

"Condemned church," Arielle pointed out.

Unforced laughter sailed past his lips. "That, it is. Nonetheless, it's still my church."

Bayfield groaned. "Just what we need, another wandering soul."

The man gestured to himself. "Body and soul intact, my friend. But more to the point, you three are drifting souls. I'm sort of a magnet to those who can't move toward the light."

Arielle gasped out, "Move toward the light! We can't be..."

Sara smoothed Arielle's hair. "I might be the source of confusion." She inched away from Arielle and Bayfield, stepping farther into the back of the church.

The man fired off several blinks before openly staring. "Now that's different."

"Then you can see the difference?" Sara probed.

He circled his hand, outlining Sara's form. "Your light overshadowed their opacity." He pressed his hands together and bowed his head Arielle's way. "My apologies. I didn't mean to startle you."

Arielle dipped her chin, accepting his apology. "What's your name?"

"I'm Father Sullivan, but everyone calls me Sull."

Arielle sized up his long hair, faded jeans, and mushroom-colored cardigan sweater. "You don't look like a priest."

"Wasn't fond of the collar, or the color black for that matter. I like being comfy."

Arielle couldn't help but giggle.

"But you can see us," Bayfield pointed out. "So you're..."

"I'll say it for you." Sull plastered a proud smile on his face. "I'm a priest who happens to be psychic."

Sara dropped the book and it hit the floor with a thud. "Thank you, Jesus!"

Sull smiled. "Amen to that."

Bayfield huffed. "A psychic priest that just happens to run into us? Come on. Are we really buying this?"

"In all fairness, you're in *my* church. We were bound to run into each other. And the Lord works in mysterious ways, my son."

"Tell that to my parents," Bayfield mocked. "They believed. Hauled my ass to church every Sunday, but God didn't stop a drunk driver from ending their lives."

Sull clasped his hands and lowered his tone. "I'm so sorry for your loss."

Bayfield offered up a gruff nod. "Thank you."

"May I have the pleasure of knowing your names?" Sull asked.

Sara spoke up first. "I'm Sara."

"I'm Arielle, and this is our skeptic, Jonathan."

Bayfield crossed his arms and huffed. "One of us has to be."

"Ignore him," Arielle grumbled, stepping between the Father Sull and Bayfield. She gave a quick glance about the room. "Why'd your church come apart?"

"My methods are a bit unorthodox." Sull took a serious tone. "I practice the belief that the Kingdom of God is inside you and all around you, not in buildings of wood and stone." A twinkle of mischief danced in his eyes. "I preached myself right out of a congregation. A church can't operate without funds, unfortunately, so I had to close the doors."

Arielle laid her hand over her heart. "That's so sad."

"For the church, yes. For the people, no. I'm filled with peace knowing they've found their connection to God, and without having to step inside a building." He kissed a silver cross hanging around his neck. "God has also kept me employed to do his bidding, but in an area I'm more suited for. I investigate religious phenomena."

His words spun about Sara's brain, piquing her interest. "Is that why you came back—to your church, I mean? Are you investigating something here?"

Sull eyed the trio. "For trespassing and breaking into a condemned church, you three certainly ask a lot of questions." He glanced down at the litter of books and papers covering the floor. "I have a few of my own. For starters, Sara, what keeps you from going into the light?" Before she could respond, he fired off question two. "And why have the two of you stepped outside your bodies?" Again, not waiting for an answer, he sounded off with question three. "And what brings you three to my church?"

Arielle nudged Bayfield, and he cast a sidelong glance at Sara, who simply offered a shrug. Bayfield let out a groan.

"Not only am I the skeptic, I'm the spokesperson." He faced Sull. "I'll get to the soul thing, but as for why we're here, we're conducting an investigation of our own and needed someplace inconspicuous to do so."

"Interesting. Investigation of what?"

Bayfield cleared his throat. "Soul stuff."

"Soul stuff?"

"Yeah."

Sull smiled. "I see. And by soul stuff, is that your explanation to my question?"

"Yes and no."

Sull regarded the three souls. Their walls were up. Getting through could pose a challenge unless he opened up first. "Priesthood runs in my family, going back a few generations. My great-great grandfather, great grandfather, and grandfather collected a large number of religious relics and documents over the years. I came back to pack it all up." He pointed toward a built-in bookshelf opposite the altar. "Care to take a look?"

Sara's eyes darted to the bookshelf, then widened. "I'm kind of a relic junky."

Sull waved her forward. "Be my guest."

Sara stood completely still in front of the bookshelf, skimming its contents. A mishmash of items cluttered the dusty wooden statues, books, journals, binders, and newspapers. A deep line cut through her forehead as she fixated and lobbed a stream of spirit energy directly at the binders, knocking them to the floor. On impact, a slew of papers escaped, skating across the wood floor.

"I'm so sorry," Sara blurted out. "I didn't mean for that to happen."

Sull waved off her apology. "I need to pack them up anyway." As he gathered up the papers and shuffled them together, a page slipped free, fluttering to the floor.

Sara's pupils enlarged as they focused on the drawing covering the sheet of paper. A book with grooves carved into leather and bound with snakeskin, held an image of a raised skull, and contained a bronze lock in the bottom right corner. Drara's book! Sara stumbled back, pointing at the drawing. "Where did you get that?"

Bayfield and Arielle rushed to Sara's side, their gazes darting to the floor. Arielle let out a squeal and grabbed Bayfield's arm. Bayfield swallowed hard, then shook off the daze. He set his sights on Sull. "That's Drara's book—the book we all signed."

Sull grimaced as he pointed down at the drawing. "You signed that book?"

"Not just us," Bayfield replied. "A house full of other people did."

Sull imitated the sign of the cross before the three mislead souls. "In the name of the Father, and of the Son, and of the Holy Spirit, Amen."

"What?" Arielle looked horrified. "Wait, why are you doing that?"

"Yes, why are you blessing us?" Sara added, duplicating Arielle's panic.

"Because we're screwed," Bayfield grumbled under his breath.

Sull presented the trio with a furrowed brow. "The book of souls is not of this realm. Its origin is one of a demonic nature. Every name written in blood will merge, giving human life to the demon possessing the book upon its completion, though the name Drara is not familiar."

Arielle's eyes fluttered closed. Shaking her head, she set her sights on Sull. "So what, like, we'd just cease to exist?"

"Indeed. Body and soul," he confirmed, his vocal pitch up a notch. "The dilemma is the status of the remaining pages. The only being who can answer this is the one in possession of the book. Without knowing how many pages are left to fill, you don't know how much time you have left; therefore, time is of the essence to locate the book and destroy it before such a time comes."

Arielle expelled a breath as if she were in pain. "I'm not ready to die. God, why did I sign?" Her gaze went to Bayfield. "Why did we sign?"

Bayfield brought Arielle into a side hug. "No one's dying." He quickly looked to Sara. "Sorry, Sara. I didn't mean to be insensitive."

"What happened to me is not your fault," she affirmed. "You two need to fight like hell."

He squeezed Arielle tight. "We're gonna fix this, make it right, I promise." His lips curled with disgust as he grinded out his words. "We're gonna track down Drara and her fucking book and destroy the damn thing." He faced Sull. "Sorry, Father, but you have no idea what we've been through. Will you help us?" Desperation bled through his voice.

Before he got a word out, Sara sprang forward and threw up her hands. "That's why we need to find Jekins."

"He's not gonna help us," Bayfield reminded her, his tone sharp.

"We don't know that. Besides, he's our best bet."

Sull inquired, "Jekins? Is that a first or last name?"

Bayfield tossed up an impatient hand and vented. "We don't know." He shot Sara a look. "How do you find a guy when you don't even know his full name?"

"Let's see…" Sull tapped his chin. "What else do you have on him?"

"He's a psychic," Arielle offered. "And he looks like the Mad Hatter."

Sull raised his brow. "Okay. Anything else?"

"The hospital," Sara blurted out.

Bayfield snapped his fingers. "That's right. He said the nurses know him."

"Which hospital?"

"Jade Forest Hospital."

"Father," Arielle softly said, "if you're willing to help us, you could go to the hospital and ask around, see what you can find out about him."

Sull smiled warmly at her while nodding. "My great-great grandfather tracked this book until the day he died. He would want me to do this, to help, to follow in his footsteps and finally destroy this evil book. I will do this for him, for the souls trapped inside this book, for the three of you."

Chapter 14

As Sull entered Jade Forest Hospital's ICU unit, Jekins's description circled the walls of his brain—sandy-brown hair, blue eyes, dressed in a tux and top hat. Arielle's statement about the Mad Hatter made sense, but he'd believe it when he laid eyes on the man. Bayfield and Arielle had also given him their room numbers, which may or may not come in handy, but he'd look in on them all the same.

His bible sat lodged under his arm and his cross visible on the outside of his shirt. Sull was no stranger to this hospital; his presence wouldn't arouse suspicion. On many occasions, he'd sat with family members, praying at their loved one's bedsides, hoping for a miracle. However, giving the nurses the third degree about Jekins may raise a few eyebrows. He needed a plan, and a good one.

At the age of five, he'd been sitting on the porch with his grandmother, drinking lemonade. She'd reached for his hand, and with her wrinkled finger, traced the longest line etched into his palm. In her shaky old voice, she'd said, "This is your path chosen by God, and one you must accept." She'd fluttered her hand about him. "The Glows follow you. This is a very special gift, child."

He hadn't fully understood what she'd meant until three years later, when he'd experienced his first psychic encounter. He'd built a fort inside his bedroom out of sheets, much to his mother's displeasure. His dog, Gus, and he had been crafting an attack against the monster army bellowing outside the tent walls, when a breeze lifted the flap entrance. Gus's hair had stood on end, and a low growl curled his jowls. A glimmering outline of a girl had appeared, sitting opposite of them. She'd wrapped her arms about her knees and whispered, "Will you help me?"

His eyes had grown round with wonder as he gazed at the girl's beautiful light. Gus bared his teeth, releasing a snarl. His eyes never left the girl as he had reached over to scratch the dog's head. "Quiet, Gus." The willingness to help had sent his heart thumping inside his chest. "Yes," he'd blurted out. "I will help you." From then on, he'd never questioned his gift or feared it. Even though religion ran in his family—that shimmering soul he'd first laid eyes on was his calling to God, what led him to priesthood, and he'd never strayed.

Sull shook off the memory, held his head high and shoulders back as he approached the bustling nurse's station. Still with no plan of attack, whatever came out of his mouth would have to do. "Good morning." He laid his bible on the counter. "I wondered if you could help me with a mission?"

The lead nurse, an older, heavyset woman with a stern brow, came to his aid. "Good morning, Father. How can I help?"

"I'm trying to track down a gentleman who may be able to help me on a lead for an investigation I'm working on." Sull gave his words a mental nod. Honesty was always best.

"Who might that be?"

"Well, I've only got a name. Not sure if it's his first or last, but the name's Jekins."

She chuckled, her whole body shaking. "He's a regular. Always visiting families of coma patients. Jekins Lipkin is his full name."

"Wonderful." Sull skimmed the area. "Does he happen to be around right now?"

"Can't say that I've seen him, but we've had our hands full today. If I see him, do you want me to give him a message?"

He handed her his card. "If you could give him my card, that would be wonderful."

"Sure thing, Father. You have yourself a good day."

"You as well."

It wasn't much, but if Jekins took the bait and gave him a jingle, it'd be a win. He'd keep his fingers crossed for that win.

Sull proceeded down the ICU hallway, following the sign directing him to rooms 400 – 420. As he reached 403, Bayfield's room, he stood quietly in the doorway, his gaze falling on a broad-shouldered man with salt and pepper hair. Music of the eighties livened up the room, as did the many mementos scattered about.

Coach glanced up, his gaze landing on the priest in the doorway. He shut off the music, pushed to his feet, and extended a hand. "Good morning, Father."

Sull gave Coach's hand a firm shake. "Good morning. How is our patient today?"

Coach sighed heavily. "No change."

"He's a fighter, this one. God is looking down on him with healing hands."

Coach's features softened and his posture relaxed. "Thank you, Father. I pray every day he will beat this."

Sull squeezed Coach's shoulder. "God hears you. He will answer soon. Keep your faith."

"I will. Thank you, Father, for stopping by."

Sull offered Coach a thoughtful expression before departing and traveling on to 410.

He viewed a bleak and depressing chamber, absence of life, and it tugged at his heart. The man and woman huddled around Arielle's bed wore haggard expressions, rumpled clothes, and disheveled hair. The sounds of whimpers met his ears, alerting him that his services were in dire need. He propelled across the threshold without permission to enter. "Good morning." He kept his tone soothing. "At times such as these, we wonder if God is listening. I assure you, he is."

The women jerked her head toward him and lashed out. "How can he be, Father? Look at our daughter! What kind of God allows a twenty-one-year-old girl to be in such a state, and at the prime of her life?"

The man held up a hand toward the woman. "Denise, please, don't start. He's only trying to help."

"Help!" A shiver of anger shook her. "Helping would be figuring out why she isn't breathing on her own, or why she hasn't woken up." She cast a piercing glare at Sull. "Can you do that, Father?"

Sull clasped his hands in prayer. *I'm working on it* flashed in his mind before he spoke out loud. "Almighty and Everlasting God, the eternal salvation of those who believe in You, hear us on behalf of Your servants who are sick, for whom we humbly beg the help of your mercy, so that, being restored to health, they may render thanks to You. Through Christ, our Lord. Amen."

Her stare hardened before she returned her focus to her daughter.

The man slowly nodded, and in an exhausted voice said, "Thank you for stopping by, Father."

His cue to leave. Sull gracefully retreated from Arielle's room. Outside in the hallway, he bowed his head and whispered, "Lord, you are the light that guides my feet. You are the map that gives me direction. You are the peace that makes me strong. My refuge and strength. Guide me in the right direction to help Arielle and Jonathan. Amen."

As he lifted his head, the edge of a black top hat disappearing into the elevator caught his eye. Sull did a double take before bolting forward and shouting out, "Hold the elevator!" The door continued to close, yet he managed to slip through the narrow opening.

A lanky man clad in a black tuxedo and top hat rattled off a sarcastic, "Out spreading the word, Father?"

Sull kept his emotions in check as he came face-to-face with Jekins, the Mad Hatter. He was certain of it. The soul of a poor young man hovered at the man's side. Sull centered on the man, and not the terrified soul, keeping his own psychic abilities hidden. The man might balk if he knew they shared psychic traits, and the fact that he was dragging off an adrift soul to God knows where. Sull threw on his acting cap. A religious artifact investigation seemed the perfect cover for his questions. "Visiting some folks at the hospital. You?"

"Same." Jekins narrowed his gaze, sizing Sull up. "I also heard you were looking for me?"

Sull spread his lips into a welcoming grin. "Jekins?" He knew who stood in front of him yet held onto the façade that he did not.

"In the flesh." He pulled out the Father's card. "Nurse Bell gave me your card."

"Very good. Do you have a moment? Can we chat?"

Jekins cast a glance at the soul beside him. "Afraid not. Got an errand to run."

Sull exuded a calm and focused demeanor. "It won't take long, just a few minutes. In fact, we've got a few while the elevator's taking us down." He didn't wait for a reply and dug right in. "I'm investigating the book of souls. You may have heard of it."

Jekins pursed his lips while shaking his head. "Can't say that I have."

"It's quite old, made from leather and snakeskin with a unique lock." Out of the corner of Sull's eye, he witnessed the young man shiver at the mention of the book.

"Like I said, it doesn't ring a bell." Jekins paused, then furrowed his brow. "Why bother with some book anyhow?"

Sull played it up, exaggerating his hand gestures, hoping to throw Jekins off his game. "It's not just some book. It's of demonic nature, possessing the power to grant human life."

Sull caught a slight stiffening of Jekins's posture, then it was gone. The soul at Jekins's side gasped out loud and stumbled against the wall. Jekins shot a "shut your mouth" look at the young man before facing Father Sullivan. He yawned, as if he couldn't be bothered. "I wish I could help. If I think of anything, I'll give you a call."

The elevator chimed and the doors parted, as did Jekins and the young man. Jekins strolled through the lobby, swinging his arms as if he hadn't a care in the world. The young man cowered next to him like a frightened animal. As they reached the hospital doors, the young man cast a horrified, pleading look over his shoulder toward Sull.

Chapter 15

Drara's palace loomed before Jekins and his passenger. He let the engine idle, not even bothering to put the car in park. He just wanted to be anywhere but there. Jekins gestured toward the front door. The poor kid huddled against the seat, his skinny arms wrapped about his torso, that horrified gaze still claiming his face. "Hey, don't let what the priest said get inside your head," Jekins encouraged. Not his usual commentary, but the kid needed to chill.

"I—I didn't sign a demon's book, did I?"

Jekins flapped a hand as he exhaled loudly. "Of course not."

The young man's eyes darted maniacally before settling on Jekins. "Are you sure?"

Jekins softened his tone even further. "Yes, now go on inside, get something to eat, and get some sleep. You'll be fine."

The young man swallowed hard, then forced his legs onto the pavement. With hesitant steps, he shuffled to the door, then glanced back at Jekins.

Jekins waved him forward, like a baby bird afraid to leave the nest. With that, the kid vanished inside, and Jekins heaved a sigh. He chucked his hat in the back seat, stripped out of his coat, and unbuttoned the first three buttons of his shirt as Father Sullivan's words bounced around his brain. Jekins twirled the Father's card between his fingers. "What aren't you telling me, Drara?" Pressing his foot to the gas pedal, he sped off, but not before calling Sull's cell.

"Father Sullivan."

Jekins gritted his teeth. *Damn it all to hell.* He had to know. "It's Jekins. I changed my mind. You got time now to talk?"

Sull's voice rose in pitch. "Yes, I do. There's a coffee shop on 5th and E Street called The Same Old Bean. You know it?"

"I do."

"I can meet you there in about fifteen minutes. Does that work?"

"I'll be there in ten," Jekins grumbled before ending the call.

****

Jekins ordered a tall Earl Gray tea, extra hot, from the darling girl behind the counter with a pierced nose and tattoo of a wolf on her forearm. She'd scribbled his name on a cup as she spread her lips into a lovely smile. He dipped his chin her way, then proceeded to wait for his tea and Father Sullivan.

Tea in hand, he spotted an empty table tucked away in the corner, perfect for a private conversation. As he took his first sip, the Father arrived, a journal of sorts tucked under his arm. Jekins shot up a hand, catching the Father's attention.

Sull acknowledged Jekins with a nod, then gestured toward the front counter as he proceeded to get a cup of Joe. If it weren't for the lid on his coffee, with an extra shot of espresso, he'd surely have doused a few folks as he zigzagged through the seated patrons pounding away on their keyboards. "I'm glad you had a change of heart," Sull said as hooked his coat around the back of the chair, then setting a leather journal on the table.

Jekins pressed his lips together in a slight grimace. "I've got a few questions about that book, Father Sullivan."

"Please, call me Sull, I insist. It can be quite a mouthful, wouldn't you say? So, the book of souls is intriguing, isn't it?" Sull chose his words wisely. If Jekins trusted him, he could be more inclined to share.

Jekins pressed his lips into a tighter, pronounced line. "Why a priest is investigating this book is what I find more intriguing, *Sull*."

Sull bobbed his head animatedly. "Yes, I guess that could be so as well."

"So, why are you?"

"Usually, a request from the church, but my great-great grandfather had an interest in this book.

Unfortunately, he passed away, and without answers. My great grandfather and father left his research untouched. I came across his journals when my father tasked me with clearing out our attic. I dove in headfirst and haven't stopped since."

Jekins leaned forward. "What've you learned?"

Sull raised his brow. "I will tell you what I know, but I expect the same."

Jekins's swinging foot suddenly went still. "What makes you think I know something?"

"A researcher never gives up their sources."

"Isn't that something a reporter would say?"

Sull dismissed the comment with a flap of his hand. "Same difference. Do we have a deal?"

Jekins lobbed a hard squint at Sull and held it there for several seconds. "Yes, we do."

Sull's lips spread into a wide grin. "Wonderful." He took a large gulp of coffee, then flipped open the journal. "From what my great-great grandfather could gather, the book dates back to the 15th century."

Jekins jerked his head back. "You can't be serious."

Sull nodded. "Possibly earlier."

"How could a book hold up over such a span of time? It would have crumbled to dust by now."

"One would think, but this book is not of an Earthly realm." Sull paused for effect. "As I stated, its origin is demonic."

Jekins waved him away and blew out a noisy breath.

"It's purpose," Sull sharpened his tone, "is to grant human life. A human would have no need for such a book; however, a supernatural creature would."

Drara flashed through Jekins's mind. "Let's say that's all true. How would a book grant human life?"

Sull sat motionless, a grim twist on his lips. "This creature, a collector of sorts, would seek out the souls of the weak, promising refuge. The price of this refuge is their signature in their own blood inside the collector's book. Once signed, the pages capture and imprison their soul." Sull observed Jekins's skin turn several shades of pale. He studied the taut expression claiming Jekins's face. Was it an admission of his knowledge of the book? Sull leaned across the table and drove it home. "The number of pages is not known to mankind, only the possessor of the book. The collector is very aware the number of blood signatures required to awaken the book's magic. When such a time occurs, every name written in blood sacrifices their soul, and they are merged into the collector, granting this creature human life."

Jekins leaned back against the chair, his gaze drifting upward, processing Sull's words. Was this what Drara was up to? She coveted human beings—their appearance, their emotions, their humanity—but stealing their soul, their life, just to be granted a human form? Jekins narrowed his gaze. "Is there actual proof, or is this just hearsay?"

Sull paused, staring down the cynic sitting across from him. He flipped open the journal, marked with a detailed drawing of the book, and slid it over to Jekins. "Is this proof enough?"

Jekins's posture slumped slightly as he did a double take. He'd seen that book once before—Drara's book. "Did your great-great grandfather sketch this?"

"He did," Sull confirmed. "In his journal, he describes the book firsthand, though a page was torn from it. I can't image why he would've done that, but as I stated, I found his paperwork in our attic. I'm certain he must have documents elsewhere. Unfortunately, that is unknown to me." He regarded Jekins with a thoughtful expression. "May I ask a question of you now?"

Jekins wet his lips before pressing them together. "A deal's a deal."

An alert gaze illuminated Sull's eyes as he asked, "Have you seen this book?"

Jekins's mouth went dry as his mind raced with worse case scenarios. What was the punishment for lying to a priest—banishment straight to hell? Then there was Drara, some sort of magical creature in possession of the book born from a demonic nature. Would her wrath be worse? Jekins shifted in his seat as he cleared his throat. "I believe in God, Father. Therefore, the only answer I can give is the truth. Yes, I have seen it."

Sull chose his words carefully, hoping Jekins would sing like bird. "A recent sighting?"

Jekins gave his head a quick shake. "Once, years back." His brain pushed play, evoking the memory. *A bloody mess that hospital had been. Multiple car pileup with souls lined up, itching to put their John Hancock in Drara's book.* "A book like that...you never forget."

"The book or its purpose?" Sull questioned with an arch of his brow.

"Purpose?" Jekins played along, knowing full well the purpose of her book.

"If you did indeed lay eyes on this book, it wasn't just sitting around on a coffee table," Sull speculated. "You witnessed a live show, my friend."

The cords in Jekins's neck stood out as he snorted in dismissive laughter. "You're fishing, Father."

Sull offered up his palms. "You came here to discuss the book, did you not?"

A scowl tugged at Jekins's brows. "I came to ask my own questions."

"And you have," Sull pointed out. "Yet I'm the one investigating the book. Did you not think I would have question of my own?"

"To tell you the truth," Jekins snapped, "I really didn't think about it."

"Fair enough. So, where do we go from here?" Sull gestured to Jekins. "You've got questions and I've got questions. Do we help each other out or not?"

Jekins crossed his arms over his chest. "Sorry, Father, but I can't help you."

"Then we're at an impasse." Sull finished his coffee and scooped up his journal. "If you should change your mind, don't hesitate to call. Good night." He pushed out his chair and nodded.

An incredulous look came over Jekins before he tipped his head to the side. *What the hell just happened* came to mind. He sat in a stupor while taking a sip of tea.

Sull hurried along the sidewalk, a sly grin claiming his face. He'd provoked Jekins's suspicion, pulling off the first part of his plan. A novice surveillance of Jekins kicked off the remainder. He'd purposely parked his car several feet away and across the street, but close enough for a clear view. The warm glow of a streetlamp spilling over the coffee house entrance only aided his plan. As he slid behind the steering wheel, gaze locked on The Same Old Bean, Sull initiated his first stakeout.

Ten minutes passed without activity. No one had come in or out, especially Jekins. Why was he still there? Jekins should have hightailed it out of there to meet up with whomever had that book.

Sull leaned forward, giving the entrance a good squint. Had something happened? Gone wrong? He lowered the driver's window and cocked his head. The steady whoosh of cars on the nearby street pierced the calm of the night. He sank farther into his seat, heaving a sigh. Surveillance had lost its appeal. He shoved the key into the ignition, just as a flash of gray fell across his vision.

That prickling sensation he'd get just before a preternatural occurrence itched across his skin. A neighboring dark force tugged at the walls of his psychic brain. Something or someone, and not of this earth, awakened his calling. Another flash of gray flickered in the distance, just short of the coffee house. Sull narrowed his gaze, homing in on an ambiguous figure gliding along the sidewalk. As it crossed under the streetlight, a crown of gray braids, glowing orbs, and a feminine form covered in armor emerged.

A sudden cold sensation spread through his gut. Sull peered closer, his face inches away from the windshield of his car. He couldn't make out her face. He was too far away, but whomever or whatever she was, just entered The Same Old Bean. He bolted out of his car. Trailing after her, he skidded to a stop just before the entrance, sucked in a few deep breaths, then yanked the door open. She stood in the center, translucent palm open, blowing glimmering dust about the room. One by one, the patrons slumped into compelled slumbers, yet he and Jekins remained conscious.

Her head of gray braids cocked, then she turned around, locking her cat-like yellow orbs on Sull. She puckered her lips and blew the radiance powder directly into his face.

Sull coughed and waved the remnants away. Her vertical pupils constricted as she studied him. "And who might you be?" she asked.

Jekins pushed to his feet, gesturing to Sull. "Drara, meet Father Sullivan." Jekins arched a brow. "Apparently, a psychic as well."

Sull fiddled with his shirt sleeves. "Ah, yes, I did leave that part out of our conversation, didn't I?"

"That, you did," Jekins grumbled.

"A psychic priest." Drara paused, taking in the meaning. "I rather like that combination."

Sull skimmed the room with a furrowed brow. "Came back to ask one more question of Jekins, but walking into this, I've forgotten what."

Drara conveyed a sigh of annoyance. "I required privacy. To most, I am invisible. If I had preceded to converse with Jekins, these humans would have perceived him as mad, talking to himself. Therefore, they sleep." Drara flapped a dismissive hand toward the spelled humans. "They will wake shortly."

"I see." Sull tilted his head and paused. "Probably to their benefit not to bear witness."

"You see a lot of things," Jekins butted in. "Like my passenger in the elevator."

Sull exchanged a knowing look with Jekins. "I did, and his horrified expression."

Jekins entered Sull's personal space. "What is it you're truly after, Father?"

Drara flashed a dismissive glance at Jekins. "We are all after something." Her orbs shifted to Sull. "Right, Father?" She didn't allow him to reply. "What I am curious about is your ease with my presence."

Sull inched closer, his eyes wide. "My investigations have led me to many strange phenomena. I do apologize if my lack of wander has offended you. May I ask what you are?"

"I am..." She paused, her gaze shifting to the silver cross hanging around his neck.

"Does my cross bother you?"

Her head snapped upright. "No, of course not." Drara pushed her shoulders back and raised her chin. "I am a collector of souls."

Sull's heartbeat sputtered with a rush of adrenaline. "Are you familiar with the book of souls?"

Her bloodless lips parted. "You know of this book?"

"Of course he does," Jekins spoke up, his tone sharp. "Can't stop asking questions about it."

Drara's eyes narrowed. "Are you asking about the book?"

"I am," he admitted.

"For what purpose?"

Sull pulled his brows in, weighing the pros and cons. He could lay it all on the line, tell them everything he knew, or give a version of the truth. "For many reasons, but most importantly, to locate it's whereabouts."

"What could a human possibly want with such a book?"

Sull scowled. "To destroy it."

Drara stood completely still, her expression blanching in surprise.

Jekins rubbed his brow, momentary muted. He glanced at Drara. Sull's remark seemed to have floored her. He'd never seen her vulnerable. Was she as clueless about the book's past as he was? Jekins quickly dismissed the thought. She knew; she had to. But that taken aback expression claiming her face was genuine. Jekins faced Sull and demanded, "Why destroy it?"

Sull lifted a single brow and raised his hands. "Did you not listen to a word I said earlier? The book is evil. Human souls are trapped inside its pages."

Jekins pinched his lips together. He didn't want to betray Drara, but it was no use. The questions flew out of his mouth, hell-bent on uncovering the truth. "Drara, why must they sign in their own blood? What truly happens to their soul? Do you take it from them? Has your obsession with becoming human led you to robbing others of their souls? Is that how you're going to accomplish a human form?"

Her yellowish orbs grew dark, and a single vein pulsed in the center of her forehead. As her lips curled, she unleashed an earsplitting screech, crumpling Jekins and Sull to their knees, hands cradling their heads. Drara vanished, leaving the front door wide open.

Jekins staggered to his feet, shaking off the ringing in his ears. Sull grabbed a chair arm, hoisting himself upright, his gaze landing on the sleeping humans just beginning to rise. He latched onto Jekins's arm and dragged him over to a table, forcing him into a seat. "Care to explain what all that was about?"

Jekins glared at Sull. "I don't owe you an explanation, but I think we're going to need each other to remedy this. That book you showed me is Drara's. She targets people in comas, they sign, and I drop them off at her palace." He shook his head. "I believed she was safeguarding their souls while their bodies healed." He clasped his hands together. "I still believe that, but her fixation with humans might have gone a bit too far."

Sull rested his hand on Jekins's forearm. "I need you to come with me. I have something to show you."

Chapter 16

Bayfield claimed a pew, arms and legs sprawled across the bench, head resting on the back, eyes focused on the ceiling. Arielle sat propped up against his shoulder, knees drawn to her chest, fingers drumming her thigh. Sara, still in research mode, squatted amid books, newspaper clippings, and photos, searching for anything that might lead them to a clue. The protesting creak of the church door summoned the trio to their feet.

Sull appeared in the doorway. "We have a visitor," he announced, waving the person inside.

Mental numbness muted Bayfield, Arielle, and Sara—not a single word was uttered between them as their incredulous stares fell upon Jekins, the man who had escorted them to Drara's. Sull gestured Jekins farther into the room. "I think you know Arielle, Jonathan, and Sara."

A grimace pulled at Jekins's brows. He slowly shook his head and quietly offered, "I'm sorry."

Sull squeezed Jekins's shoulder. "God forgives." He bobbed his chin toward the three souls peering at Jekins with saucer-like eyes. "We must as well."

Bayfield forced down the burn of anger rising in his throat and kept his tone neutral. "If you're here to help, that's all that matters."

Sara flattened her lips and firmly admitted, "I can't forgive so easily." Her voice grew shaky. "That book didn't save me. I died."

Sara's words slammed into Jekins's gut. He stumbled back, searching for balance. "My God. I didn't know."

Arielle delivered a feisty accusation. "I'm not buying it, Jekins. You're her driver. You rounded up two hundred souls for her. You had to have suspected something."

His gaze darted between them. "Why? I had no reason to."

Sara hands clenched several times before she spoke. "So you just drop people off and never look back?" She didn't wait for a reply. "Drara was at the hospital when I died. She told me she would fix it. That witch put a mind warping bug inside my brain! For five years, I sat mute, helpless, a victim of her ruthless magic."

Jekins clasped his hands in a begging fashion. "I'm so sorry. I didn't know. Yes, I knew she coveted humans, wanted to become one. I knew the power of her magic—the book's magic. But I had no idea of the risk each soul put themselves in by signing it." His voice rose. "I don't think she did either, and I completely trust her. Drara has protected every soul she's encountered. I never dreamed... I fully believe her intent wasn't to rob humans of their souls."

Sull pushed his hands in a downward motion. "Let's all take a breath. There's no doubt there's a lot at stake, but we need to work together. Prior to coming here, Jekins and I confronted Drara. We spooked her and she vanished, which makes our task of confiscating the book all the more difficult."

"You met her?" Arielle blurted out.

He opened his mouth, but Jekins held up his hand, cutting him off. "Drara can't carry out her plan alone. She needs a human to perform earthly tasks." He heaved a deep sigh as he looked to the floor. "She vanished because I hurt her."

Sull asked, "But will she return?"

"I'm certain of it." Laying a hand against his breastbone, Jekins added, "I know her. She's not evil. She wouldn't harm anyone."

Sara laughed. "Ah, hello, she stuck a bug in my brain to shut me up. I'd say that's dreadfully evil. If she didn't want people to find out the truth, she shouldn't've allowed them to leave that mansion of hers."

Jekins offered up some possible theories for Drara's reasoning. "When you tell someone they can't have something, don't they want it all the more? Maybe your death threatened her...her plan. Forgive me, I'm not trying to make excuses for her. You must remember, she's not human. She doesn't think like we do. Everything's black and white to Drara."

Sara made a tsking sound.

Jekins nodded. "Yes, what she did was wrong. It was awful, inhumane, but to her, maybe it was protection. She's lonely. She wants to experience compassion, love, acceptance."

Arielle pretended to rub her eyes. "Oh, boohoo. Give me a friggin' break, Jekins." Her voice rose. "She lied, used us, and all for her own gain. No matter how you spin it, it was…"

"Fucked up," Bayfield finished for her.

"Jekins has a point." Sull held up his hands, warding off the commentary. "Drara is not human. We can't possibly understand her motives. Besides, we need her on our side. Without her cooperation, our chances are slim to none of obtaining that book." He turned to Jekins. "Do you know how she acquired the book?"

"I have no idea."

"Do you have any idea of her age?"

"I just know there were several others before me doing her bidding."

Sull frowned. "The book dates back to the 1400s. I find it hard to believe Drara was its original owner."

Arielle gasped. "Did you say 1400s? That's, like, ancient."

Sara tapped her chin. "There should be some sort of history reference,"—she glanced at Sull—"other than your great-great grandfather. A book like that, and that old, should have a past."

"Maybe we're looking at this all wrong," Bayfield spoke up. "If the book's that old, its pages would have surely been completed by now. What's stopping it? Why haven't we gone up in smoke?"

Arielle gave Bayfield's shoulder a good nudge. "Speak for yourself."

"Surmising here." He returned his attention to the group. "Shouldn't it have done whatever it's supposed do many years ago? Are we even talking about the same book?"

Jekins cut a rigid hand through the air. "No way there's two books."

Sull agreed. "It would be hard to assume there's more than one, but Jonathan does bring up a valid point. Why hasn't the book accomplished its goal?" He quickly faced Arielle. "Not that we want it to, of course."

"What happens when you Google it?" Sara put before Jekins and Sull. "What sites, images, or facts come up? It could be helpful."

Jekins offered Sara a stern look. "The internet is not your friend."

She waved his remark away. "Seriously, what does it say?"

Sull laid his hand on Arielle's shoulder. "I don't want to upset Arielle with Google's findings."

Arielle rolled her eyes. "I'm not a child."

"Really?" Bayfield teased, giving her a squeeze.

"Let it rip, Father."

Bayfield looked down at Arielle. She had a habit of spinning out. Whatever Sull was about to spill, there was a ninety percent chance Arielle would freak. To be on the safe side, he kept his arm around her.

"Google had a lot to say, mostly fabrications," Sull offered up, "such as the book of sinners, granter of eternal youth, the skeleton's key, the grim reaper's journal, the book of death. I could go on and on, but there were two that rang true: the binder of souls, and the book of souls."

Arielle shuddered under Bayfield's arm. He kissed the top of her head and pulled her into his side. "Just nonsense, Arielle."

"Yeah."

Jekins spoke. "We need Drara."

Sull raised his brows. "We do indeed. How do we find her?"

"Watch the ICU wards. She's always on the lookout for her next signer."

Chapter 17

Dr. Marcus stood in the doorway of Bayfield's ICU room, observing Coach humming to eighties rock while glued to Bayfield's bedside. He tapped his knuckles against the frame, drawing Coach's attention. "Heard you wanted to see me?"

Coach switched off the tunes and waved the doctor inside. "Yes." His eyes shifted briefly to Bayfield. "Dr. Yoo says Jonathan's making progress, but he never elaborates on the details." He sized up the doctor. "You seem like a straight shooter, so I'm asking: how's Jonathan, really?"

Dr. Marcus tucked his hands into his lab coat's pockets and rocked back and forth on his heels. "Dr. Yoo is right. Jonathan's recovering nicely. His brain function continues to improve, and the swelling is minimal."

"All good news," Coach admitted with a nod, "but why hasn't he awakened?"

"The truth?"

"Yes, absolutely."

"With these stats, he should be awake. It's a bit puzzling as to why he's not."

"Puzzling," Coach repeated, voicing wonder. "No one in this hospital can tell me why?"

"Dr. Yoo is the best in his field." Dr. Marcus gave Coach's shoulder a sympathetic squeeze. "Jonathan couldn't be in more capable hands. Dr. Yoo has discussed Jonathan's case with his colleagues. We just don't have an answer."

"I've tried everything to reach Jonathan, but nothing changes." Coach massaged his temples. "I just wish I knew if any of it was working."

"We don't know that Jonathan isn't responding to everything you're doing," Dr. Marcus advised, but also encouraged, "Yet it could be a large contributor to his progress."

"I hope you're right."

"Has Dr. Yoo discussed taking Jonathan off the ventilator?"

Coach snapped his head upright, his eyes wide. "You want to take him off? What if he stops breathing?"

"Then we put him back on the ventilator."

Coach chewed his bottom lip, mulling it over. He wasn't a risk taker, and even more so when it came to family. The pros and cons had to line up perfectly, and with far more pros than cons. Here things weren't black and white as he liked them. A huge gray spot stared him straight in the eye.

"He's ready, Mr. Meyers," Dr. Marcus conveyed.

Coach locked his arms over his chest and stared the doctor down. "How positive are you that nothing will go wrong if you take him off?"

A confident gleam lit up his eyes. "Fairly certain." He raised his brows and added, "However, there can be risks when taking an unconscious patient off a ventilator."

"Such as?"

"Labored breathing. A reduction in blood oxygen levels. An increased amount of blood returning to the heart. Overloading the circulation and causing heart failure. The brain not receiving sufficient oxygen. Renal fail—"

Coach let out a gasp and interrupted. "And you still want to take him off?"

"I do," he stated, his voice firm. "Staying on the ventilator long-term can be more risky and harder to come off of as the body becomes dependent on it. We'll carefully monitor all his vitals. If he shows any adverse signs, we'll put him back on the ventilator."

Coach shifted his stance from one foot to the other. He'd asked for the truth, and the doc gave it to him like a fist in the gut. Lying in that bed was no life for Jonathan, and he would want to take the risk. For Jonathan, he had to do the right thing. "Can I be with him when you take him off?"

"Of course, and it won't be an ICU nurse. Dr. Yoo and I will handle it."

A dark cloud washed over Coach's vision. As it cleared, his eyes shifted to Jonathan, lying motionless and tangled up with tubes. He faced Dr. Marcus. "Yes, let's try."

"You made the right decision." Dr. Marcus gave a curt nod, approached the door, and stopped to add, "Hang tight. Dr. Yoo's on rounds. I'll go hunt him down."

Coach's gaze lingered on the empty doorway before circling back to Bayfield. "It'll be okay, buddy." He rubbed his tired eyes, then stretched his arms overhead, fighting back a yawn. "I'm gonna grab a cup of coffee while we wait for the doctors. I'll be right back."

The coffee station claimed the far-left corner of the ICU. Families of ICU patients gathered around its curved counter multiple times a day, as the caffeine provided that much-needed pick-me-up, as well as the chance to chitchat. Coach thought it only fitting to give it a nickname. *The Watercooler* fit the mark. As he trucked down the corridor, the rich aroma of dark roast filled the air. Approaching the station, he inhaled a good healthy breath of coffee, then spotted Carey, Arielle's father, stirring cream into a hefty glass of steaming black coffee. Coach grabbed a mug off the shelf and nodded. "Morning, Carey."

Carey lifted his glass in acknowledgement. "Coach. Beautiful day outside. Wish the kids could see it."

"They'll get there," Coach reassured him.

"How's Jonathan doing?"

Coach added a touch of cream to his coffee, followed by a mountain of sweetener. "The doctors say he's improving, but he hasn't woken up yet. Now they want to take him off the ventilator. Makes me nervous, but I gave 'em the okay. What about Arielle? How's she doing?"

Carey gave an understanding nod of his head. "Same story here, but then, Arielle came off the ventilator yesterday—"

Coach didn't let him continue and blurted out, "Is she awake?"

Carey stood still, his eyes glazed over. "She hasn't woken."

Coach's gut clenched. "I'm so sorry, Carey. I just assumed—"

He waved his free hand in the air. "No need to apologize. Both our kids are going through this." His expression brightened a bit. "She's breathing just fine on her own, and all her vitals look good, so that's good news." Carey reached for another glass and poured a second cup of coffee.

"Yes, it is." Coach glanced at the second glass. "How's Denise?"

Carey sighed. "It's been tough on her. I can't get her to leave Arielle's side, not even to get something to eat. She's determined to be there when Arielle wakes. They haven't always seen eye to eye. They got into a quarrel right before the accident. Denise is carrying that guilt."

Coach offered Carey a thoughtful expression. "It'll work itself out."

"I'm staying positive."

"I am as well."

Carey edged away, then stopped and faced Coach. "Don't worry. Jonathan will do fine off the ventilator."

"Thank you, Carey."

"Until our next cup."

A faint smile touched Coach's lips. "Yes." He watched Carey drag himself down the hall and vanish into Arielle's room. Taking a sip of coffee, he pressed forward. The chime of the elevator rang in his ears. As the doors parted, Dr. Marcus and Dr. Yoo stepped into the corridor. Coach sucked in a deep breath and steeled his nerves before following them into Jonathan's room.

"There are a few things I want to make you aware of—" Dr. Yoo began in his soft-spoken voice.

Coach cut him short. "Dr. Marcus gave me the candid rundown."

Dr. Yoo narrowed his gaze at Dr. Marcus.

"I informed Mr. Meyers of the risks," Dr. Marcus confirmed.

Dr. Yoo's smooth complexion grew taut. Coach assumed Dr. Marcus stealing the show had something to do with that look.

"Very well." Dr. Yoo's voice lacked its usual composure. He cleared his throat, reclaiming his rigid mannerism. "We will switch to an acute weaning method, SBT."

"SBT?"

"Spontaneous Breathing Trial," Dr. Marcus clarified.

"Yes." Dr. Yoo continued. "To be successful, he must have a respiratory rate of 35 breaths per minute, and a heart rate of—"

Coach held up a hand, halting Dr. Yoo. "While I appreciate you explaining the procedure, I'd rather not know the details and leave them to you, if that's okay."

Dr. Yoo studied the anxiety carving lines into Coach's forehead. "Yes, of course. However, I feel I must ask once more. Do you have any questions?"

Questions? Sure, he had a shitload of them. He just wasn't prepared or ready for the answers, and he wanted to get this over with, like ripping off the band aid. "No questions."

Dr. Yoo nodded. "Let's begin." He faced Dr. Marcus. "CPAP mode, pressure support 5 – 8 cm H2o. We'll start with 30 minutes." The machine's hum diminished.

Coach gripped Bayfield's hand. "I'm right here, buddy." He leaned over the bed railing, fixing an intense stare on Jonathan's chest. He observed no sputtering, gasping, or puffing, just calm, even breaths. An ultra-awake feeling rushed through Coach's body and he laughed out loud. His gaze darted to the doctors and landed on the puzzled expressions plastered on their faces. He rubbed a hand over his mouth, wiping away his smile. "What is it? What's wrong?"

Dr. Yoo gave a slight shake of his head. "That's exactly it, nothing is wrong. It's like he…"

"Was never on the ventilator," Dr. Marcus finished for him.

Chapter 18

Jekins arrived at Sull's house just after eight in the evening. He breathed in deeply before tapping his knuckles against the solid mahogany door. It swung open before Jekins's hand reached his side.

"Any news?" Sull blurted out. "Forgive me. Good evening, Jekins."

Jekins dipped chin in acknowledgement. "Father." He peered over the Father's shoulder and into the house. "Afraid not. Where's the three musketeers?"

"In the dining room, searching the internet, certain to find something I'd missed on the book."

"Sara's on a computer?"

"Yes. One of my laptops."

He offered up a blunt, "She's dead," as he sliced a hand through the air. "That pretty much seals the deal on the body-soul-energy connection thing. How's she even attempting to strike a keyboard?"

"Apparently, there's some kind of energy of the spirit persuasion," Sull explained before holding his hands up. "Don't ask."

Jekins cocked his head. "Hmph. You'd think we'd have known about that, us being psychic and all." He stared off in the distance, then shook off the puzzlement. "Taking the three souls into your home was a generous act. Better than hanging out in that rundown church of yours." He made an apologetic hand gesture. "No offense."

"None taken." He waved Jekins through the doorway. "Come inside."

Jekins pursed his lips. "Seeing we might get the trio's hopes up. Best we chat outside."

Sull joined him on the porch, leaving the door slightly ajar. "Four days with no sign of Drara. Is that normal?"

"No, it's not." A deep line etched into Jekins's forehead. "I've summoned her by thought, kept an eye on the hospitals she frequents, and not even a blimp on my psychic Richter scale. With new patients popping into the ICU, she should've been all over that."

Sull tapped his knuckled against his lips. "Could she have left? Moved on to a different city?"

Jekins shrugged. "Anything's possible." Then he axed the comment. "But don't see that happening. We have a bond, a friendship. She wouldn't just up and leave."

"What are we going to tell Arielle, Jonathan, and Sara?"

A sudden chill pinched Jekins's flesh, kickstarting his psychic radar. "Do you feel that?"

"I do." Sull pulled up his shirt sleeve. "My skin's crawling with goose bumps."

"It's Drara," Jekins announced, his voice rising an octave. "I can feel her."

"Agreed."

A dark form emerged inside the cluster of trees guarding Sull's front lawn. As it drifted closer, beams of moonlight exposed Drara's bronze armor. The neatly trimmed, wet grass smooshed beneath her boots as she approached the pair. She stopped halfway, locking her yellowish orbs on Jekins and Sull.

Jekins's shoulders curled over his chest as he laid eyes on the creature he served. "Forgive me, Drara. I should never have said those things to you."

She stood tall, shoulders back, chest out, letting her voice rise. "I will not surrender my book to either of you."

Countless souls flipped through Jekins's mind like a deck of cards. He'd escorted them to Drara's palace. He had a responsibility to save them. "Even at the expense of human lives?"

Drara retreated several steps.

Sull gripped Jekins's shoulder. A look conveying secret knowledge flashed between them before he faced Drara. "May I approach?"

Her gaze narrowed, yet she bowed her head in agreement.

Laura Daleo

Sull advanced slowly, Jekins following close behind. "I am very intrigued by your book." He came to a standstill, leaving a safe distance between them. "I'd like to ask some questions about it, if I may?"

"You may," she agreed, her stance guarded.

"Thank you." He took a few steps closer. "Has it always belonged to you?"

"The book has had many owners." She looked up, and then back to him. "Upon my birth, my creation, it was given to me. I am to carry out its purpose."

"Given by who?" Sull quickly added, "And how many before you?"

"I do not know," she simply said.

Sull regarded Drara with extreme mental focus. "Why is the book passed down to the many? Why not just the one?"

"I have no knowledge of the why."

He threw out another direct question. "The past owners, did you know them or know of them?"

"No," she replied, and didn't elaborate further.

Jekins stood quietly, feet planted to the ground, hands clasped behind his back. For now, this was the Father's show, and the commentary was far too entertaining to interrupt.

Sull tried a different approach. "Drara, can you tell me what you *do* have knowledge of?"

A condescending smile touched her lips. "The book requires signatures from unguarded souls—souls who have entered my kingdom. Its pages require blood to awaken its magic."

He furrowed his brow as he threw a pointed question at her. "How many pages are left to fill?"

She smirked and slipped the skeleton key inside her armor.

Sull's posture slumped slightly as he accepted her refusal to respond. "Very well. If you succeed and meet the book's requirements, will it grant you a human form?"

Drara's smile wavered. "I believe it will."

"You seem hesitant."

She cocked her head as she considered his words. "I do not know how to answer your question."

Sull's heartbeat throbbed inside his throat as he stretched out his hand. "Drara, may I see the book?"

Jekins's head perked up as he shot a glance at Sull, grinning as he thought, *Bold move, Father*.

Sull held up his hands in a submissive fashion. "I only want to look, to understand what it's asking of you. I will not take it from you."

Drara's pupils constricted and enlarged several times as she calculated his request. His apostolic practices could be of some value to the book's message and to her mission. The reward outweighed the risk. She swirled her right hand, producing the book, while a glowing ball of light sat in the palm of her left hand. "I will not hesitate to strike should you go back on your word."

He laid a gentle hand on her shoulder. "Your weapon is not necessary. You have my word as a priest, I will not take it from you. I merely want to examine it for my great-great grandfather."

The sphere dimmed, and then it was gone. Drara slipped the skeleton key into the lock. Her posture stiffened as she laid the book in Sull's hands. "I am trusting you."

"You have my word," he repeated as he ran his fingers over the leather. "Quite impressive."

"May I?" Jekins asked of Drara.

Drara slowly nodded.

Jekins peered over Sull's shoulder. He'd seen the book once from afar, but never up close and personal. The leather appeared as living skin: soft, supple, with a pulse of its own. Jekins scooted a step away. "That's all the glimpse I needed."

Sull held his breath as he raised the cover. The many signatures collided with his vision, no doubt written centuries ago, yet the blood glistened as if wet. At a slow pace, he flipped each page, his gaze darting back and forth, skimming over the names. "This is like nothing I've ever seen."

"Or want to see again," Jekins chimed in.

Drara snatched the book away, tucking it under her arm, where it vanished. "It has revoked your viewing."

Sull backed away, holding his hands up. "The book spoke to you?"

"Not in words. I feel it."

He stood still, his mouth slackened, taking a few deep breaths before speaking again. "Well, thank you for allowing me to see it, yet there's something nagging at me. The others that once possessed the book, what happened to them? Did the book grant them a human form?" He didn't wait for a reply as he waved his question away. "I don't see how that could be possible, as the book requires completion before awarding a human form."

Drara's gaze clouded. What had happened to the others before her? Were they promised a human form and then denied upon failure to complete the task? Would she be denied as well? With a blink of her eyes, she dismissed the doubt the Father had planted inside her brain. "I have no knowledge of the past. I can only speak of the present. It is not my place to question it or its magic. I am here to serve, and I *will* be rewarded."

"And your reward is a human form?" Sull speculated.

"Yes."

Jekins wedged himself between Sull and Drara. "Drara, you do understand the book will cause the death of many, don't you?"

A shudder ran through her. "You are mistaken. My magic protects..." Her brows lowered. "It protects them."

Jekins eyed Drara. The questions had taken their toll. He and Sull were pushing too hard. Time to zip it. Jekins looped an arm around her shoulders. "I think Drara's had enough questions for one night."

"Yes, enough," she confirmed. "This was not the purpose of my visit. I came only to inform you that I cannot allow the book to be destroyed."

Sull gave a curt nod. "Understood." Just then, his cell phone rang. "Oh, I'm sorry, I have to get this. It's my dad." He swiped the screen. "Hello, Dad?" His brows came together. "Hang on, slow down. Yes, yes, of course. I'll be there shortly." Sull slipped his phone back into his pocket. "My apologies. I've got to head over to my dad's." He trotted toward his car parked in the driveway. "He's rambling on about some envelope."

Jekins waved him away. "Of course, go."

As Sull's car backed onto the street, Jekins gestured toward his own car. "Drara, I'm heading home for a cup of tea. Will you join me?"

Her hand pressed against her throat. "You said hurtful things to me, Jekins. Things one should not say to a...friend."

His hands fell to his sides as a pained look tugged at his face. "You're right, I shouldn't have said them. I was in the wrong." He clasped his hands. "Please, accept my apology. I've truly missed your company."

Her yellowish orbs grew bright. Human emotions entangling the heart caused mortals to do foolish things. Jekins was human after all, and suffered from this defect. She brushed her fingertips across the hard metal surrounding her chest. Something thumped beneath her armor, a heart of sorts she supposed, and it desired forgiveness for Jekins. "I accept your apology, dear human."

A slow smile spread across his lips. "Thank you, Drara." Bobbing his head toward the street, he coaxed, "Come, let's have some tea. Yes, I know, you don't require tea, so just relax by the fire and chat with me."

"Very well."

As Jekins opened the passenger door, he said, "By the way, where do you keep that book? It's not like you've got any pockets in all that armor."

Her eyebrows drew together as she stared at him.

"It's a joke, Drara." He shook head and closed her door. Sliding behind the wheel, and before pulling away from the curb, he cracked a smile. "If you want to become human, you must understand humor."

"Humor?"

"Yes. Something that makes you laugh. Brings joy. Makes a lousy day better."

"Ah, yes," Drara said, a far-off gaze taking hold. "I have not experienced humor." She cocked her head to the side, her braids falling along her shoulder. "The souls I govern have never shown me humor, only sadness, pain, and fear."

Jekins gave a heavy nod. "You got dealt a hard hand, Drara."

"What does that mean?"

He waved it off, glancing at her out of the corner of his eye. "You know, I ran into someone the other day." He paused, debating. "I ran into Sara Clark."

She jerked her head toward him, her memories conjuring up the soul he referred to. "That is not possible."

"Well, I did, and she's..."—he raised his brows—"...dead, her soul just wandering around."

A blank look filled Drara's eyes before she repeated, "That is not possible."

He struggled with calling her out, but he had to force the issue for Sara's sake. "She says you gave her something that messed with her brain, left her mute and crippled for five years." He angled a hard squint her way. "Five years, Drara."

"Yes, I am aware of her death. I was with her. She wanted me to fix it, bring her back to life." She looked at him then. "I could not give her that. I gave her a magnet."

"A magnet?"

"A spirit magnet." A blank look came over her. "The magnetic pull should have fused her body and soul as one, allowing her to be released from the book and move one. Failure would only occur if my instructions weren't followed."

Jekins shrugged. "Well, failure occurred, and big time. That magnet turned into some kind mind-wrapping creature. What saved her was leaving your palace. The real world turned that bug into mush."

She lowered her head. "My purpose is not to cause suffering. I am the soul collector," she said out loud, as if to substantiate it. "I govern them, not harm them." Drara fixed a fervent stare on Jekins. "Do you believe me?"

He did a double take. The Drara he'd known for so many years was not the wide-eyed, hands clutched together, vein bulging in the center of her furrowed brow sitting across from him now. He felt her conviction in his bones. "Yes, Drara, I believe you."

Chapter 19

Arielle pinched her lips together, releasing a muffled groan. "I'm done. An hour and a half of surfing the internet is redonkulously frustrating." She glanced at Sara. "You've been at it for, like, four hours. How are you not sick of it?"

Bayfield bobbed his head in agreement. "I've got Arielle beat by ten minutes, and she's right. Centering all my energy on finding trauma patients is exhausting."

Sara snickered. "So is a relationship. You two oughta think about that." She pushed the laptop aside. "But you know what? I do need a break. Gonna see what Sull's up to." She left Arielle and Bayfield with incredulous stares plastered on their faces.

Arielle's eyes widened as she looked at Bayfield. "Do you think we're a...."

"Couple?" Bayfield finished for her.

"Yeah."

He reached for her hands. "In my head, yes, we're definitely a couple."

She couldn't stop the smile from spreading on her lips. "I feel the same. I know it's only been a short time, but seriously, this whole mess has been so hard, and it feels like it's been a lifetime. We've stayed sane because of each other."

He blinked. "Hard? Nightmare is more like it." He smiled with his eyes. "But you here with me, I can deal. You're the best thing that's ever happened to me."

Tears welled up in her eyes, and she gulped down a breath. "And you for me. You've grounded me, let me see what's important in life."

As he stood in front of this beautiful soul, Bayfield tried to calm his racing heart, but it was pointless. His gaze drifted to the soft, supple curve of her mouth, and he slowly leaned forward, capturing her lips in a kiss. His soft, fiery, but gentle lips drew Arielle closer, pressing her body against his, wanting to be trapped in this moment forever. The need to breathe pulled them apart.

"What happens to *us* when we're back in the real world?"

Bayfield held her at arm's length, searching her eyes. "Why would that change anything?"

Arielle pressed her hand against her breastbone. "It won't for me, never...ever."

"Me either." He rested his forehead against hers. "You complete me. I could never be with anyone else. You're the one, Arielle."

"You're my everything, and you're stuck with me."

They're lips smashed together with a fervent urge.

Sara barged into the room and sounded off, "Where the hell is Sull?" Caught up in her conundrum, their kissing hadn't registered in Sara's brain. "He's just gone!"

Bayfield parted from Arielle and came to Sara's aid. "Maybe he had a church thing."

"Maybe, but he didn't mention it. Don't you think it's weird he would just up and leave?"

"Should we check the church?" Arielle offered.

"Sull didn't want us roaming around and getting into trouble," Bayfield reasoned. "That's why he brought us into his home."

"You're right. Best we stay here." Sara rubbed frown lines in the middle of her forehead. "It just feels odd."

Bayfield shrugged. "We don't really know him. Maybe this is just normal for him."

"Maybe." Sara's voice came down a notch.

Arielle guided Sara over to the dining room table. "Jump back on the computer. Searching sites will take your mind off of Sull."

Sara didn't say another word as she plopped down in front of the laptop and flipped it open. Bayfield and Arielle settled into chairs on either side of her, watching the monitor. The force of energy flowed from Sara's fingertips and onto the keyboard, driving the keys hard, and pulling up yet another site. A dark vortex of screaming souls plastered across the leather binding of an ancient book flashed on the screen.

Sara flinched and jerked away from the laptop, while Arielle latched onto Sara's arm, her eyes bulging.

Bayfield's reflexes kicked into protector mode as he closed the screen and pushed the computer away.

"Oh my God!" Sara blurted out, flipping it back open. "That looks like our book, but worse!"

Arielle agreed. "A thousand times worse."

Bayfield deliberately lowered his head to stare, then gathered his brows. "Screaming souls sucked into an oblivion of darkness wasn't on the book I signed."

"But everything else is the same," Sara argued in a shrill tone. "The leather, the lock, the size." She scrolled down the page. "And look at the pages—the signatures in blood!"

"Calm down. We don't know for sure it's blood," Bayfield pointed out.

"What are the chances there are two books out there?" Arielle challenged. "We have to consider this may be our book." She turned to Sara. "When Sull gets back, we have to show him this."

Sara gave a quick bob of her head.

"Agreed," Bayfield replied. "He's the expert."

Chapter 20

Sull swung the car onto his father's driveway, shoved the gearshift into park and killed the engine. The large dumpster on the front lawn, loaded with debris from the remodel, caught the corner of his eye. "What a mess," he mumbled as he trekked up the porch steps. He announced his arrival with several raps on the front door before swinging it open.

His father sat perched on the edge of the sofa, gripping a large dusty envelope in his lap. As he met his son's eyes, he sprang to his feet, waving the envelope in the air. "The construction crew found this when they tore down the kitchen wall."

"Dad, what's this all about?"

"It's your great-great grandfather's. That missing page from his journal."

Sull gripped the cross around his neck. Surely this wasn't a coincidence. God had a hand in the envelope popping up at such an appropriate time. "May I see it?"

His dad claimed a spot on the sofa, then patted the space next to him. "You'd better sit down."

Sull eased onto the cushions, his posture rigid, his eyes locked on the envelope. His hands trembled as he pulled out the sheet of paper. He glanced at his father before his eyes traveled to the dark ink scribbled across the discolored page. At a frantic pace, his eyes flicked over his great-great grandfather's words. A sudden chill ran through him, and his stomach twisted into knots as the final sentence met his gaze—*God help us all.* It sank into the walls of his brain, conjuring up worst-case scenarios—eradication, torture, starvation, corruption, despair. "Lord help us," he murmured, just as an image sketched below the writings fell into his sightlines. He studied the two heart-like vines sprouting from the base of a figurative cross, coiling up its post and spreading into wings. Was it a sign, a clue, something that would save the world? Sull's lips parted, and the paper fluttered from his hand, floating toward the floor. Everything he'd believed was wrong. He snatched up the page in midflight and scrambled to his feet. Throwing open the front door, he faced his father. "I'm sorry, I have to leave." Without waiting for a reply, he raced to his car.

Sull gunned the engine, whizzing down the driveway and onto the street, his free hand drumming the steering wheel, waiting for his Bluetooth to connect. As the connection flashed on the navigation screen, he commanded, "Call Jekins."

After two rings, Jekins answered. "All good with your pops?"

He disregarded the concern for his father and rattled off, "Meet me at my place, ASAP! Find Drara. It's imperative you bring her with you."

"Drara's here, with me." His tone rose. "What's happened?"

"I'll explain in person. Everyone needs to hear this, especially Drara."

****

Sull bulldozed through his front door, his gaze colliding with an empty living room. He charged forward and into the dining room, skidding to a halt in front of the souls gathered about the oval dining room table. He held up the sheet of paper. "You have to see this!"

In concert, and overlapping Sull's words, Sara, Arielle, and Bayfield echoed, "You have to see this!

In unison, all four blurted out, "What?"

Sull heaved an exaggerated breath. "Fine, you three first. Show me."

The trio frantically waved him toward the open laptop in front of Sara. Sara pointed at the screen. "We found this." The pitch of her voice climbed a notch as she added, "I think it's our book."

Sull stooped down, his face inches from the monitor. Countless souls, eyes wide in terror, screamed in torment as they spiraled into a black hole. He jerked back. "My great-great grandfather was right. The book has deceived all who have come across it."

"What do you mean, all?" Bayfield swallowed hard as he gestured to himself, then Arielle, and then Sara. "Like us?"

Sull observed the souls before him, a serious expression pulling at his brows. "Unfortunately, yes."

Arielle's eyes blazed. "You need to spill, Father."

Several taps on the front door interrupted his reply. He held up a finger. "And I will, right after I answer the door." He hurried off, vanishing from the room.

"I have a bad feeling about this," Bayfield remarked.

Arielle shuddered, then hugged her arms. "God, I wish I could go back in time and erase my name from the damn book."

Sara agreed. "I second that."

Approaching footsteps steered the trio's attention toward the entryway. Sull appeared with Jekins, yet they weren't alone. Drara drifted past the men to stand in the center of the room. Her yellowish orbs narrowed as she recognized three of her wayward souls.

Facing the Father, she demanded, "What is the meaning of this? Why have you brought me here?"

Before Sull could offer an explanation, Bayfield tossed a glassy stare at Drara. "Yeah, why the hell is she here?"

Arielle sneered. "Hasn't she done enough?"

Sara crumpled to the floor, trembling. Bayfield and Arielle helped her into a chair.

Sull raised his voice. "Everyone in this room is essential, including Drara."

Sara found her voice and lobbed her accusation. "She killed me."

Drara whipped her head in her direction. "I did no such thing."

Sara sprang to her feet, knocking the chair backward. Her fingernails dug into her palms as she shouted, "Yes, you did! Your magic didn't protect me. I died. You were there, remember? You promised to fix it." She leveled her gaze. "Instead, you had me swallow some creature who destroyed my brain." Spit flew from her mouth. "It left me mute and crippled for five years!"

Drara threw her shoulders back and her orbs grew fierce. She towered over Sara and breathed out words in a surprisingly composed tone. "Did you follow my instructions?"

"Of course I followed your rules. I waited until I was inside your palace before I swallowed the bean."

"I gave you five simple words to repeat: 'Of one soul and body.'" Drara paused, identifying the flaw. She fixed a stern gaze on Sara. "Did you repeat them before swallowing the magnet?"

A blank expression took hold of Sara. Her eyelashes fluttered with several blinks before she uttered, "I forgot to say them. Oh, God, this was all my fault." Sara cupped a hand over her mouth, muffling an uncontrollable whimper.

"Yes," Drara agreed. "It was."

Jekins shook his head. "Drara, she knows. Let it go."

Drara continued to deflect blame. "I was accused of something I had not done, nor would I."

Jekins took Drara by the shoulders and forced her attention away from Sara to him. "I know that." He bobbed his head toward the others. "Now they know it too."

Sara's arms hung heavy, pulling her shoulders low. Her voice lost its power as she spoke. "I'm sorry." Her eyes quickly left Drara's and traveled to Bayfield and Arielle. "I misled you. Drara did instruct me to speak those words. I forgot. I caused my own suffering."

"Hold up, Sara." Bayfield jumped to her defense. "This isn't on you." He jutted a finger at Drara. "Your magic was supposed to keep us alive. Wasn't that the whole damn point of signing that book? This shouldn't have happened."

"My magic has done exactly that; although..." Drara paused, and turned her back on Bayfield to face Jekins. "I have not been truthful," she confessed. "Yes, others have met the same fate as Sara, though not because my magic failed." Her voice grew soft. "Their age became too great. Their loved ones had perished. The world was no longer as they knew it. I did for them as I did for Sara. I released them from the book and let them move on and into the light."

Jekins laid a hand on her shoulder. "Thank you for telling me."

"No one's safe," Sull interrupted, his tone strained. "Not even the souls you thought you released, Drara." He held up the torn page from the journal. "This is the reason you're all here."

Jekins's lips twisted into a downward grimace. "Is that what I think it is?"

Sull gave a curt nod. "Yes, the missing page from my great-great grandfather's journal. The information I had gathered and discussed with all of you was inaccurate. The book was not what I had originally thought."

Drara spread her lips into a proud grin. "As I stated, you were mistaken."

Sull raised his brows. "Yes, and you as well. However, not in the way you think." He began to read. "These are my great-great grandfather's words: *My research has led me astray, or the cunning nature of the book has thrown me off course. The many who have served this book, enchanted by the promise of a human form, have also been fooled. A human form could not be further from the truth. These loyal creatures, though none grasp what they are truly harvesting, have gathered its crucial signatures in hopes of a reward. None are the wiser, yet I have triumphed over its deceit. The book is nothing more than a farce, a hoax, a method to achieve a plot. Peeling away its layers of disguise, I have managed to uncover its true face, its true purpose, far from its promise to its followers. The book seeks power, control, domination over mankind. Its completion opens a gateway hidden beneath its leather, releasing all evil onto the Earth—an apocalypse of the vilest kind. Life as we know it will end. Darkness will fall. Humans will become slaves. The book must be destroyed—its course of destruction halted. Ancient drawings depict the hope of salvation. I must believe a savior moves among us, one courageous enough to cause the downfall of the book. My knowledge of its true intent must be safeguarded, for if this page were to fall into the wrong hands, hands loyal to the book... God help us all.*"

He caught his breath, then placed the sheet of paper on the table. "If the book is not destroyed, souls will continue to drift while their bodies remain earthbound. Whomever has signed will never awaken." He glanced at Sara. "Or enter the afterlife." He squeezed his eyes shut, muttering, "And God help us all if that book gets what it needs and completes itself."

Silence engulfed the room as they stood motionless, mouths gaping, expressions blanching, thoughts scrambling to understand. It was Drara who backed away, objecting, "No. These are merely words on paper."

"Look at the monitor," Sara urged, waving Drara over. "These souls are screaming in pain. The book *is* evil!"

Drara peered at the vortex of shrieking souls, her pupils fluctuating. Flashes of her birth lit up her brain. Was she created for this, to torture? To inflict pain? What of the souls she released? Was the promise of a human form a charade? Would she remain in this despicable form forever, a slave to the book? Drara's pale skin grew mottled. A guttural roar raced up her throat. In a burst of magic, she fled the house, vanishing into the dark night.

Jekins stood in the open doorway, his hands gripping its frame. "Drara, no! Come back!"

Sara rushed past him and into the street, screaming, "Drrraraaaaa!"

Sull grabbed his car keys before dashing out of the house, pulling Jekins along with him. "Come on, Jekins, we have to find her."

Jekins jumped into the passenger's seat as Sull gunned the engine. As the car spun onto the street, it screeched to a stop inches away from Sara. Jekins rolled down the window and shouted, "Sara, get inside!"

Sull echoed, "Get inside. Stay with Arielle and Jonathan. We'll be back soon. And don't worry, we'll find her." In the rearview mirror, he watched her form vanish inside the house, then returned his eyes to the road. "We'd better find her," he aimed at Jekins.

Jekins furrowed his brow. "You said that like you think I have some control over it."

"I know you don't. Besides, she couldn't have gone far."

Jekins jerked his head back. "Seriously?"

"What?"

"It's not like she travels by car. She pops in and out like a damn genie. She could be anywhere by now."

Sull tossed him a hard stare. "Not helpful."

"Sorry, but it's the truth."

"Well, where would she go?"

"Hmm..."

"The hospital?"

Jekins shot the idea down. "Not now. She wouldn't have the stomach for it." He pressed his fingers to his temples. "Give me a minute."

"What about that palace of hers? Would she go there?"

"No can do. Any solid matter would be ripped to shreds, human or creature."

Sull pursed his lips. "Does she have a house of sorts? Some place she stays?"

"Not that she's mentioned. Can you just give me a second to think?"

"Well, she's got to go somewhere," Sull rambled on. "She can't wander the streets. Would she want to be around people, or someplace quiet perhaps?"

"Father!" Jekins snapped. "Zip it! I need silence to sense her presence. With your jabbering, I can't concentrate."

"Yes, of course." Sull simulated zipping his mouth shut with his fingers.

Jekins settled into his seat, letting his mind go blank. That dark hue of psychic energy crept into his brain, growing fuzzy with chatter from departed souls. In misery, they begged him for a glimpse at their loved ones. Jekins sifted through their white noise, searching for Drara. The voices retaliated, shouting for attention. He deprived them of acknowledgement. His mission was Drara.

Sull kept his mouth clamped shut while focusing on the road. Inside his head, he told himself, *we'll find her*, repeatedly, never allowing a sliver of doubt to creep in and persuade him otherwise. The alternative wasn't an option.

Jekins groaned. "I'm not getting anything." He cocked his head, casting a sidelong glance at Sull. "We should channel our energy."

"Excellent idea." Sull, yanking the steering wheel hard to the right, tossed Jekins against the passenger door.

Jekins grunted, and then sneered. "Whoa, where's the fire?"

"Apologies." He gave Jekins a quick nod. "Had to catch that turn. There's a park just down this street. We can park there and join forces."

"Well, let's not get killed before we get there."

Sull eased his foot off the gas pedal. "Right."

A cluster of treetops peeked between the gray clouds scattered about the night's sky. The parking lot housed several cars, and pedestrians strolled along the park's well-lit walkways. A beautiful night to the unsuspecting public. Sull parked farthest from the crowd, shut the engine off, and reached out his hand to Jekins. "Let's find her."

Jekins gripped his hand and closed his eyes. Sull followed suit. Their minds joined as warriors, drifting into the afterlife and awakening cries of despair and hopelessness. Fragments of colored glass shimmered between the hovering souls. A tall building unfolded from the darkness, the colored glass setting into its frame. An arched rooftop caught a beam of moonlight, shining upon an irony cross. Double arched doors swung wide open, illuminating wooden pews, an altar of stained glass, and the many parishioners, Drara being one of them.

Sull's eyes flew open, a deep frown settling along his brow. "I know that church. Lady of Angels. Why would Drara go there?"

Jekins stared off in the distance, shaking his head. "I have no idea."

"I can't speak for an immortal being, but humans go to church for several reasons: worship God, teach their children about God, become better people, or in times of trouble or sorrow."

Jekins waved his hand in a forward motion. "What are you waiting for? Let's go find out."

For the third time that night, Sull gunned the engine before skidding onto the street.

Chapter 21

Jekins and Sull barged through the church doors, interrupting mass and turning heads. Quite a few scowls flew their way before the churchgoers returned their attention to the service.

Sull dipped his fingers in the basin of holy water, making the sign of the cross. Jekins echoed his actions, then shooed him forward.

"Do you see her?" Sull whispered.

Jekins scanned the pews, catching sight of her gray braids. "There, three pews up and on the right."

Sull followed Jekins at a quick pace. Before the pew Drara occupied, they both genuflected and made the sign of the cross before entering. She sat toward the middle, alone. Her yellowish orbs made contact with them, then shifted to the bibles stacked in a shelf of the pew in front of her.

Jekins scooted past her to sit on her right, with Sull on her left. Jekins quickly skimmed the faces in the crowd. All eyes were directed toward the alter. He spoke in hushed tones as not to draw attention from the parishioners. "Drara, you do understand this is a church, right?"

She pulled her head upright, laying eyes on Jekins, then briefly meeting Sull's. "This is where human's go to beg for favors, is it not?"

Sull cracked a smile. "I guess that's one way of putting it." The pitch of his voice was just above a whisper. "We come to worship, or pray, or rejoice."

"Is there something you want to ask God for, Drara?" Jekins probed.

She rubbed the heel of her palm against the armor over her chest. "There is a strange heaviness here. One I have not felt before."

Sull rested his hand on her shoulder. "A feeling of sadness, perhaps."

She blinked. "Sadness?"

Jekins waved them both away. "Never mind that, Drara. You've come for a favor...what favor?"

Her pupils constricted into vertical slits. "If the book is truly evil, I fear it must be destroyed, and in doing so, I will also perish. I want to live, even if I must remain in this form. I am here to beg for my life."

Jekins's mouth fell open. The creature he'd served most of his life departing from his world had never occurred to him. He'd grown to love her. Not in a romantic way, but as a daughter or a sister, someone he'd protect at all costs. He took her pale hands in his, squeezing them tight. "I won't let that happen. We'll find a way to do both." He shot Sull a pleading look. "Won't we, Father?"

Sull offered up his hands. "Take my hands and let us pray." He gripped their hands firmly, yet muted his tone. "Lead us not into temptation, Lord. Deliver us from evil, for Yours is the kingdom and authority and glory, and I desire to live for Your kingdom, not the enemy's."

Drara's eyebrows came together, her tone uncertain. "Will that keep me alive?"

Sull smiled warmly at her. "We must have faith that it will."

"Come back to the Father's with us," Jekins urged. "Let us free you from this burden."

Drara eyed the men on either side of her as she considered her options. Cooperation meant nothing if the book defended itself. To her knowledge, a challenge had never occurred, or if it had, its advisory's fate had been one of doom. Though she had been created for the book, it had not created her, and had never interfered in her decisions. She knew the power of her magic, yet could it stand up against such an evil force? If she did nothing, would the book simply replace her with one willing to do its bidding at all the costs? And if they succeeded, flooding the earth with evil, what would become of Jekins? For Jekins, she had to try.

"Yes, dear human, I will go there for you."

****

Sull and Jekins escorted Drara into the living room, which once again sat empty. "They must be in the dining room," Sull said, waving Drara and Jekins forward.

Drara crept along, her shoulders curling over her chest, her gaze distant. Knowledge of the book's true intent shattered everything she believed. What was her purpose, her fate? Had it always been to destroy the very book she'd been created for? Would annihilation of the book slay her as well? Her fingers curled about the skeleton key, squeezing tight as her focus became clear—survive.

Sull entered the dining room, followed by Jekins, and then Drara. His guests sat staggered about dining room table, their glum faces fixated on the torn page of his great-great grandfather's journal, still lying in the center. Recognition that he and the others had returned put it on pause.

Bayfield caught movement out of the corner of his eye, and then tapped Arielle's arm. In unison, they rose to their feet, eyes wide and locked on Drara.

"Drara," Sara uttered, pushing out of her chair and rushing toward her. "Thank you." Sara pressed her hands together in prayer. "Thank you for coming back."

Drara dipped her chin in acknowledgement, then turned her back on Sara and faced the Father. "What is it that I must do?"

Sara backed away and claimed a spot between Bayfield and Arielle.

Sull took stock of the entire room before his gaze settled upon the oval table. He spread his hand on its smooth surface, his fingers pushing aside the torn page. "Why don't we start with the book." He patted the wood. "Here's a good spot."

Drara scowled at the simple sheet of paper responsible for the chaos. A pained breath caved her chest before it rattled past her lips. With a lackluster wave of her hand, she brought forth the book. Its unearthly presence shifted Drara's focus, and she ran a finger over its leather like a caress from a lover.

Jekins rested a hand on her shoulder. "I understand," he softly said.

Sull studied the ominous book with a narrowed gaze. "As a priest, it's quite appalling. As a researcher of relics, I'm in awe."

"Wait," Arielle spoke up. "We're forgetting about all those people inside Drara's palace."

Her gaze darted across their faces. "What happens to them? Shouldn't we warn them?"

"She's got a point," Jekins concurred. "We cook this book, we end them too."

"Those people don't care," Sara ground out. "They won't leave even if you warn them. The real world no longer matters to them."

"We should warn them anyway," Bayfield advised. "It's only fair they know what's coming."

Drara's hands briefly clenched before she offered up her veined palms. "And what warning would we give? The outcome of its destruction is unknown."

Jekins offered up a shrug. "The thing didn't come with instructions. We don't even know how to destroy it."

Sull pursed his lips. "My guess is holy water."

"You have holy water just lying around?"

Jekins's comment sent a bark of laughter flying out of his mouth. "I'm a priest. Why would I not?"

Jekins tipped his head as if he were wearing his top hat. "Touché."

Bayfield went into full boxer mode, throwing a few quick jabs into the air. "I say we douse the book with it. A whole bottle if you have it."

Sara thrust her fist in the air. "Agreed. Drench the thing."

Arielle shuddered, then brushed the goose bumps off her arms. "You're acting like we're just squashing a bug. We all should be totally freaked out."

Sull held out a trembling hand. "I am." He glanced around the room. "I think we all are. It's okay to be frightened."

Drara huffed, then laid the skeleton key next to the book. "Am I opening it or not?"

Jekins's breath quickened as he grabbed Drara's arm and pulled her back. "Does everyone agree that the book isn't going to just sit there and let us destroy it?"

Drara locked eyes with Jekins. "In all likelihood, it will defend itself." She glanced at Sull. "We should be prepared."

"Prepared for what?" Bayfield blurted out before pulling Arielle into his side.

In a calm, steady voice, Drara replied, "For the worst."

Sara waved a hand toward the table. "It's a book. What's it going to do?"

Sull pushed his hands in a downward fashion. "Hang on, now. Drara and Jekins make a valid point." He gave a nod toward Sara. "You as well. Yes, it's a book, but an evil one at that, and one filled with magic."

"Maybe we should test a single page," Sara offered up.

Sull jutted a finger out and wagged it at Sara. "Yes." He presented her with his most compassionate priest expression, yet he directed his words to Drara. "Do you know the page Sara's signature is written on?"

"I do." Drara unlocked the book and held her hand over it, flipping pages with inhuman speed. They fluttered to a stop three fourths of the way through. Drara tapped the paper just above the bottom. "There."

Sull's eyes never left Sara's as he ripped out the page. "Are you ready?"

Sara's hand clasped her chest. Her page was *the* test. Would its destruction send her into the light or leave her earthbound? She was already dead, no harm no foul if something were to go wrong. "Yes, I'm ready."

"Wait!" Arielle caught on, rushing to Sara. Knowing she couldn't hold her, she mimicked a virtual hug before her arms sank straight through Sara. "I'll never forget you, Sara," Arielle murmured."

Sara's voice grew soft as she said, "Nor I you." She looked over Arielle's shoulder, finding Bayfield's eyes. "Take care of her."

"You know I will," Bayfield assured.

Sara centered her energy around Arielle, squeezing tight and hoping she felt it. A breath hitched in her chest as she let go and approached Sull. "Let's do this."

Sull nodded. "I must gather what's needed." He vanished down a hallway, then the creak of a door disturbed the silence. Several minutes passed before footsteps drew near and Sull emerged, gripping a silver tray. Upon its polished metal lay an antique cross, three vials of water, and a thick bible. Sull set the tray opposite the torn page, and in a formal fashion, he prepared the items before praying, "Dear God, in the name of Jesus, I ask that You come against these demonic influences. I know you have the miraculous power and strength to conquer the darkest enemy, break the strongest barrier, and silence the greatest deceiver. Your name is Worthy, Glorious, Almighty in power, and I claim victory today in Your name. Send Your mightiest warriors to fight this battle. Lord, shine Your light upon us, free us, and pull us back from the enemy's grip. Amen." He tipped the vial over Sara's name. The drops sizzled like cool water splashing on sweltering asphalt.

Drara expelled a gasp, her chest caving into her stomach. Brilliant light bled from her palms, swirling into flaming balls.

Sull ignored the threat, pressing his thumb against the coarse paper and rubbing out Sara's name.

Jekins snapped his fingers in front of Drara's face. "Hey, Drara, neutralize the firebombs."

"I am doing the best I can." Drara's limbs shook as she defied the book's demands to strike. "The book is reacting, not me."

"You lob those and the whole house goes up in smoke," Jekins pressed.

A low growl passed her lips as she spoke. "I am aware."

"Then turn off the fireworks."

"Quiet, human!" she snapped. "I cannot concentrate with you jabbering in my ear."

"Oh my God," Sara cried, holding up her hands immersed in a white glow. The shimmering radiance spread beneath her flesh, peeling away layers of her existence.

"It's working!" Jekins shouted, his eyes darting between Sara and the fireballs in Drara's palms.

"The light of God surrounds us." Sull's voice grew higher as he jammed his thumb onto Sara's written name, rubbing frantically. "The love of God enfolds us. The power of God protects us. The presence of God watches over us."

Bayfield's hands fell to his sides as he locked his eyes on the lit-up Sara.

Sara's eyes sparkled one last time, before her human form splintered into blinding light and vanished from the human world.

Arielle cupped a hand over her mouth, suffocating a hopeless wail.

The firestorm continued its rage inside Drara's palms, the rumbling force lifting her off the floor. Her veins bulged against her flesh and a muffled howl slipped over her tongue. "I will not set this priest's house ablaze!" Drara channeled every ounce of strength into her hands, commanding her magic to annihilate the flames and disable the book's power. The infernos hissed and scurried like ants across her palms before dimming like a lightbulb, sparking for the last time. Her empty palms flashed before her eyes. She blinked and looked again. Only her translucent pale flesh fell into her range of vision. A gasp of relief rushed from her lungs as she slumped into a chair, her arms dangling at her sides.

Bayfield hung his head, closing his eyes. "It's over."

Arielle skimmed the room, sobs gripping her chest and spilling onto her cheeks. Sara was truly gone.

Jekins knelt beside Drara, resting a hand on her knee. "You did it."

"Yet we have more to do," Sull advised, interrupting their moment of victory. His wild-eyed gaze shifted to Bayfield and Arielle. "We shall test your pages next."

"Give it a beat, Father," Jekins retorted. "Drara's exhausted." He tossed a hard squint at the book. "We keep ripping out pages, things are going get a lot worse."

Even in her weakened state, Drara held her chin high. "I am fine. I want to continue."

Sull fixated on Drara, a depiction burning behind his eyelids of the creature pouring holy water over the very book she protected. "Drara, I think it is you who has the power to destroy the book."

Jekins's mouth hung slacken before he snapped it shut and got to his feet. "That's insane."

"Is it?" Sull disagreed. "She was created for the book. She just might have the power to stop it."

Jekins entered Sull's personal space. "And what if it kills her?"

Sull gripped Jekins by the shoulders. "I don't think it will. It retaliated through her to attack an outsider, a threat."

Jekins stepped away, shaking his head. "Anyone who attempts to obliterate that book is a threat—you, me, and even Drara."

Drara used the table to push her body upright and face the Father. "I have no more power over the book than anyone in this room. It will rage war on whomever threatens its existence."

"I suggest we conduct another test." Sull pressed the issue. "Have Drara tear off a corner and see what happens. At least we'd know."

"Sounds too risky," Jekins advised.

Drara settled the debate by grabbing the book. Devoid of emotion, she ripped the corner from the first page. Sparks ignited, spewing embers off the aged leather and engulfing her hand into an orange blaze.

Sull dashed into the kitchen, seized a dish towel, and drenched it with water. With large strides, he bolted toward Drara, her shrieks ringing in his ears.

"Chuck it," Jekins called out, his hands in the air. Sull lobbed the soaked towel like a football, and Jekins snatched it out of the air. He draped the soothing cloth about Drara's hand. "It's okay, it's okay," he cooed, patting out the flames before casting a scowl at Sull. "Got any-more bright ideas?"

Bayfield tuned out the chatter, his gaze homing in on the page displaying the cross with heart-like vines. Something about the drawing nagged at his brain, dredging up an old memory. *He had been about seven, sitting on a church pew, his parents on either side of him. His mother had been on her knees, hands clasped in prayer, tears staining her rosy cheeks. His father had slumped against the pew, an unfocused gaze claiming his eyes. The baby brother or sister that had been inside his mother's belly had left them. No one knew why, it just was. He had sat very still, watching his mother and father, not knowing how to help them. His mother had glanced over her shoulder and caught him staring. A smile brightened her wet eyes. As she slid back on the seat, she had squeezed his hand and whispered, "You're my anchor, the strength that keeps me grounded."*

Bayfield shook off the memory, then snatched the sheet of paper off the table. He shoved the drawing in front of Sull. "She needs an anchor."

Sull squinted, then frowned. "What?"

"An anchor," Bayfield repeated. "Something to keep her grounded." His gaze darted to Drara, then back to Sull. "If, as you say, she's to destroy the book, but not herself along with it, she'll need something to keep her bound to our world—the human world."

Sull snapped his fingers. "I think there was something about an anchor in my great-great grandfather's journal." He swept the journal off the bookshelf and thumbed through the pages. "Ha!" He pointed to the page and read aloud. "The souls scribbled across its pages anchor the book to the human world. Without their signatures, the book has no power, no magic."

Jekins scoffed. "How does that keep Drara from getting scorched?"

Sull cocked his head as his gaze flicked upward. "I'm not sure."

Bayfield thrust himself into the conversation. "What if the drawing isn't just vines and a cross."

Arielle bobbed her head in agreement. "Like a symbol for something."

Bayfield arched an eyebrow and clarified, "Or someone."

"Yes!" Sull agreed. "My great-great grandfather's sketch could have been a depiction of an anchor." He gestured to himself and Jekins. "We could stand on either side of Drara and become her anchors."

"Hate to throw a wrench into your plan…" Jekins pursed his lips and gave a slight shake of his head. "But I was standing beside Drara when her hand burst into flames. And you, Father, were a close second."

Sull rubbed his forehead as if to ward off a headache. "This is true." His gaze circled the room, and then landed on the journal. "The souls are the anchors." As the meaning behind the statement became clear, it swiftly prickled his flesh. "The souls are the anchors," he repeated, then slowly faced Bayfield and Arielle, his eyes bright. "The souls are the anchors!"

Jekins sighed heavily. "You keep saying that."

He leveled a hard look at Jekins and tapped his temple. "But do you understand what I'm saying?"

Jekins took stock of Sull's expression. The stern lines etched into his brow lobbed the answer into Jekins's brain. His gaze darted to Bayfield and Arielle. Were they Drara's anchors? Would they protect her and keep her tied to the human world as the book was destroyed? Jekins let out a long, low sigh. "There's a huge *if* in that theory, Father."

Drara's orbs constricted as she studied the two men. "What theory?"

Jekins looked away and to the floor, shaking his head. He couldn't bring himself to tell her.

Sull quietly informed her, "When the book is destroyed, we believe you must have a soul on either side of you—ones who have signed the book—making contact with your flesh. Without these anchors, you will be destroyed, along with the book."

A wave of awareness cooled Drara's flesh. The very souls she'd urged to sign, with the promise her magic would protect them, would ensure her survival. She'd failed them. None had reason to help. She broke into a restless stance as the ability to see a positive outcome drifted away.

Bayfield detected a flicker of fear in the confident, proud creature. She faced the possibility of death, something she probably never imaged a reality before now. Whatever evil created that book had used her too. Why should she have to die? Yes, she rallied its signatures, and for her own gain, but in his heart, he truly believed she had no intention of harming anyone or had knowledge of the book's true intentions. She just wanted to survive. So, wasn't she a victim as well? He pushed his shoulders back and stepped forward. "I'll do it."

Drara jerked her head in Bayfield's direction, an incredulous stare claiming her face.

"Thank you," Jekins uttered.

"No!" Arielle cried, rushing toward Bayfield. "What if something happens? What if something goes wrong? What if you never wake up, or worse? Don't do this."

He cupped her face in his hands. "You're stuck with me, remember? I'll make it through this, I promise."

She clutched his hands and frantically shook them. "You can't possibly know that. No one knows what's gonna happen when that book gets hosed."

"You're right, we don't, but this needs to end." Bayfield offered her a sad smile. "And honestly, I really want to go home." He caressed her cheek. "I want to see you, touch you, introduce you to Coach and my life. I have to do this."

His words softened her anxiety, melted her heart even, but there was no way he was leaving her side. "Then I'm going with you."

Bayfield tossed his head from side to side, shaking it adamantly as he sliced a hand through the air. "No way. Absolutely not. It's too risky."

Arielle rested her hand on her hip and sized him up. "So, it's okay if you go, but not me? Well, hell to the no on that. We do this together. I'm going. End of story."

Bayfield gripped her shoulders and lowered his head. "I want...*I need* you to wake up. I couldn't live with myself if anything happened to you, Arielle."

"You just told me you'd make it through this," she threw back at him in a fierce tone. "Now, suddenly, because I say I'm going, it's too risky?"

He ran his fingers over his head, before interlocking them in a begging manner. "I can't let you do this."

"I'm not asking, and *you* can't stop me from going." She marched over to Drara and shoved her palm into the air. "Drara, high five. Let's do this!"

Drara forced a smile as she lightly touched her palm to Arielle's. "Silly human gesture."

Bayfield charged forward, mouth open in protest, but Sull blocked his path. "Jonathan, we don't have the luxury of a choice in this matter. There must be two souls. Arielle is the second."

Bayfield's eyes pleaded with Sull as his hands fluttered at his sides. "There are hundreds of souls at Drara's palace. Ask one of them to be the second anchor and spare Arielle, please!"

Drara offered a half-hearted shrug. "Only you, Arielle, and Sara chose to abandon its walls, not the others. This is your cause, not theirs. This world is meaningless to them. They have what they want. Why would they leave now?"

Arielle slipped her fingers between Bayfield's and held on tight. "I'll be okay. We'll be okay. We can do this, together."

A visible shakiness came over him as he laid his hand over her heart. "I love you, Arielle."

Her eyes grew bright and glossy. "And I love you, Jonathan."

Chapter 22

Sull nodded toward the two remaining vials of holy water. "Drara, you'll pour both vials over the book as I recite the prayer."

"Good thing you live out in the boondocks, Father," Jekins conveyed, and he was dead serious. "No one around to witness the hullabaloo."

"I'm a priest who investigates religious relics," Sull pointed out the obvious. "I chose this house for its discretion and distance to avoid that very scenario. I'm confident there will be no interruption."

"Well, that's one thing in our favor." Jekins cast a scowl at the book. "If I never speak of that book again, it would be too soon."

"You?" Bayfield huffed and spread his arms. "Arielle and I are the victims here. What are we waiting for? Let's get this over with."

Drara released a noisy breath. "No more talk. Jonathan, join me and Arielle so we can end this."

Arielle slipped her arm under Drara's and locked onto her with a firm grip. "Ready." She squished her brows together. "Well, sort of ready." She gave a firm nod. "No, I'm ready."

Bayfield took his place next to Drara and hooked his arm about hers. His eyes found Arielle's. "Can't wait to see you."

"Me too." A smile touched her lips and as her gaze shifted from Bayfield to the book, the creepy thing sent a shudder of fear through her, obliterating her smile.

Drara snapped her fingers. "Father, give me the vials."

Uncertainly flickered in his eyes. "Maybe we should perform a test first."

"Enough with the tests. You are stalling now out of fear." Drara stuck out her hands and waved her fingers toward him. "The vials, now."

Jekins snatched them up and placed them in her open palms. "Be safe."

She acknowledged her human with a nod.

Sull held up his hands and recited the same prayer. "Dear God, in the name of Jesus, I ask that You come against these demonic influences. I know You have the miraculous power and strength to conquer the darkest enemy, break the strongest barrier, and silence the greatest deceiver."

Drara flipped her wrists, dumping both vials of holy water and dousing the book. The aged leather crackled as dark smoke seeped from its pages.

Sull's voice bellowed as he continued. "Your name is Worthy, Glorious, Almighty in power, and I claim victory today in Your name. Send Your mightiest warriors to fight this battle. Lord, shine Your light upon us, free us, and pull us back from the enemy's grip. Amen."

Bayfield tightened his grip on Drara, his knuckles growing white. "Arielle, hold on tight. Don't let go."

Arielle smashed her body against Drara's and clung to her arm. "Not letting go."

The book flipped on its side, sizzling, popping, and hissing in protest before bouncing across the table, spewing thick smoke. Bright orange sparks ricocheted off the leather, snapping the book in half and engulfing it in flames.

Sull sang out in prayer, louder this time, and lifting his hands to the heavens. "Almighty Father, there are evil forces around us that we cannot battle by ourselves. But by Your strength and Your power we are saved. Give us strength, Oh Lord, to fight this battle, for with You all things are possible."

Inhuman screams billowed inside the swirling inferno, simultaneously awakening the stench of rotting flesh. A sudden surge of heat rumbled the house's foundation. The floorboards bowed and splintered as the dining table thumped and skidded upon the wooden floor, threating to cave and plunge everything and everyone into the pits of fiery Hell. Unearthly wind howled about Drara, Bayfield, and Arielle, wedging its icy fingers between the trio.

Arielle pressed her face into Drara's chest, clamping her free hand over her ear, mouthing, *"Oh my God."*

Bayfield's mouth hung open, his eyes wide and transfixed on the horror unfolding. "Jesus."

Jekins stumbled, searching for balance, and latched onto the kitchen archway, his gaze darting to Drara. An aura of luminous magic looped about her as she stood tall, invincible, arms locked about her two souls, orbs narrowing into slits and glowering at the book.

Flames exploded like gunfire, soaring upward and spreading a brilliant white-orange blaze over the ceiling, yet nothing burned, the holy water's mission very clear—destroy only the book. Its broken, scorched pieces floated inside a powerful vacuum marked for death. A surge of heat blurred the room, thundering into a massive explosion, obliterating the book's remains.

Drara cocked her head, listening to the eerie quiet. Was it a warning? A signal of what's to come? The teleportation? She pulled Arielle and Bayfield close, her grip fierce.

The unnatural gale reawakened, whooshing about the trio, lifting them off the floor and thrusting them into a spiraling funnel of darkness. Arielle's screams echoing throughout the room faded to an unnerving quiet as the trio suddenly vanished.

"Drara!" Jekins shouted, dashing to the spot where she'd stood.

Sull spun in a circle, his gaze scanning the room. "Did it work? Where did they go?"

Jekins fell to his knees and cried, "They're gone, destroyed with the book!"

Sull scooped him off the floor and gave him a light shake. "We don't know what happened, and there's no time to fall apart. We'll find them." He released him and surveyed the room once more. "Jonathan and Arielle may have returned to their bodies."

Jekins ran a hand through his hair, muttering, "If Drara didn't make it, I'll just..."

"Don't think like that," Sull voiced strongly. "As I said, we don't know anything yet. I'll go to the hospital and check on Jonathan and Arielle. You stay here in case they return."

Jekins nodded as a harsh breath rattled past his lips.

Chapter 23

The rotating passageway into the unknown decelerated, and heartlessly discarded Drara, Bayfield, and Arielle onto a spongy platform, circling like a merry-go-round. Drara sprang to her feet, with Bayfield and Arielle nestled in her arms, and gathered her sense of balance. Her pupils constricted, adjusting to the darkness and taking in the tiny specks of light flickering above and beneath them.

"Where are we?" Arielle whispered.

Bayfield stretched his hand out in front of him, feeling his way while keeping a tight grip on Drara. "This doesn't feel right."

Drara yanked him back and ordered, "Stay close." She surveyed the fairy lights dancing throughout the dome. Two broke free from the starlit cluster above and descended downward. Her gaze narrowed, observing the way in which they traveled with a deliberate intent toward Bayfield. An icy chill spread over Drara's flesh as she sensed their true essence. With purpose, she released Arielle's hand, throwing her back into the rotating passageway. The vacuum sucked Arielle's body upright, thrusting her toward the edge of the platform.

"Jonathan!" Arielle shrieked before tumbling over the rim and completely vanishing.

"Nooooo!" Bayfield screamed, and shoved Drara away with his free hand. "Why did you do that? Why did you let her go? I have to help her. Let go of me." He glanced at the spot Arielle had stood and wailed her name into the darkness, "Arielle!

Drara tugged him closer. "Quiet! Relax, I merely sent her on her way." With her free hand, she lifted his chin, forcing him to look up. "It is you they wish to speak with, not her."

Bayfield resisted, clamping his chin downward. "You have to let me go after her, please!"

"Jonathan." A beautiful voice filled his ears, silencing his cries.

Bayfield froze, goose bumps shimmying down his spine. He knew that voice! His head jerked upward. "Mom?"

Two glistening lights floated toward him. As they landed, the lights shifted. Hundreds of tiny stars scrambled together into the likeness of his mother and father, their bodies glittering in the darkness. His mother drifted a step closer. "We altered your course and brought you here, to us."

Bayfield squeezed his eyes shut, shaking his head. "This isn't real."

"They are very real," Drara said in his ear. "Look at them."

Bayfield raised his eyes. His parents, twinkling like diamonds, stood inches from him. Sobs gripped his chest as he stumbled back, searching for balance. Drara swayed with him before steadying them both. Bayfield struggled to free himself from her grip, anxious to embrace his parents.

"Letting go will send you on your way and end any chance of communication with your parents," Drara warned him. "I can let go if that is what you want."

He quickly shook his head. "No, don't let go."

"Very well," she said, bobbing her chin toward his parents.

Bayfield faced them, shuddered, and swallowed a gulp of sorrow. "I don't understand...What is this place? Is this where you went after you died?"

His mother smiled that smile he'd seen so many times before. "No, honey, we went into the light." She looked about the dark dome. "This is an opening in time, a gathering if you will, for souls spanning realms. We couldn't let you reach earth before seeing you, speaking to you."

"We're so proud of you, son," his father said, "and of Coach. He has been a wonderful parent in our absence. We are so grateful and thankful to him."

Bayfield's eyes bounced back and forth between his parents, his mouth gaping, his voice mute.

His father gazed at him, an affectionate expression beaming across his face. "We've watched you blame yourself for the accident. We came to tell you it wasn't your fault."

"But it was my fault," Bayfield blurted out, finding his voice. "I missed my bus. You had to drive me to school. It's my fault."

"No, son, it isn't," his father assured. "We could spin this several ways. I fell back to sleep after my alarm when off. I got a late start which made you late, so I could say it was my fault as well."

"Or mine," his mother spoke up. "I didn't wake either of you. I wanted to give you both that extra time in bed while I relaxed with a cup of tea on the porch."

His father rested a luminous hand on Bayfield's shoulder. "So you see, it could have been any of our faults, but the one true person responsible was the drunk driver."

Tears spilled down Bayfield's cheeks. "I d—didn't know all t—that. I thought..."

"We know what you thought," his mother conveyed. "We've been waiting all this time to tell you." She kissed his cheek. "You are my anchor, Jonathan, and you always will be."

His father kissed his other cheek. "Forgive yourself. You did nothing wrong."

Bayfield blubbered and crumpled to his knees, dragging Drara down with him.

His mother knelt beside him, her glowing hand caressing his tearstained cheek. Warmth flooded his body as she spoke. "Remember, I'm watching over you from above." She kissed his cheek once more. "It's time to go back home, my sweet boy. You're going to have a beautiful, happy life."

Drara opened her hand, releasing Bayfield and sending him on his way.

Chapter 24

Arielle's eyes fluttered open. A stark-white hospital room fell into her line of vision, and the constant beep of a monitor irritated her ears. Her mother and father sat at her bedside, looking sad and haggard. Her brain sat in a thick fog, blurring perception. "Mom? Dad? What happened?"

"Arielle!" Denise cried. "Oh my God." She turned toward the doorway and shouted, "She's awake! My daughter's awake!"

An army of nurses swarmed the room, surrounding Arielle's bedside. The lead nurse ordered, "What's her stats?"

A nurse cuffed Arielle's arm, squeezing the life out of it, while another stuck a thermometer in her mouth, and a third placed two fingers at her wrist.

"Blood pressure's 90/60."

"Pulse is 65."

"Temp's 98."

Arielle's parents huddled together, eyes wide, expressions pulled taut.

"I'm fine," Arielle protested, pushing the nurses away. She glanced at her parents, the fog beginning to lift. She'd fallen off their boat and ended up here. Catwoman's yellowish eyes and her creepy book flashed inside her head. She'd signed that book! Then the Mad Hatter showed up to take her to some fairy-tale palace. Was it all a dream? But it felt real, super real. Her eyes swept the room and shiver ran through her as the present resurfaced. "Oh my God, Jonathan!"

"Jonathan?" Denise questioned.

"Yes. Did he make it?"

Denise turned to the lead nurse with a look of concern.

"You've just woken up, and there can be some disorientation or confusion," The lead nurse stated. "Calm down. Take a deep breath."

"I'm fine," she said again, louder this time. "I'm not confused or disoriented. I'm just asking about Jonathan."

Denise frowned and leaned toward her husband's ear. "Jonathan who? She can't be asking about Coach's Jonathan. They don't even know each other."

He gave a quick shoulder shrug, his gaze glued on his daughter.

"Do something," she ordered her husband.

In his authoritative *money talks* tone, he barked out, "Get Dr. Yoo in here, now!"

The head nurse leveled her gaze, as if to challenge his request, then gave a curt nod. "Yes, Mr. Robbins."

She left in search of Dr. Yoo, along with two of the nurses, while one stayed behind to monitor Arielle. The nurse approached Arielle's bedside, and in a soft, soothing voice, asked, "What's Jonathan's last name?"

Arielle blew out a gasp of relief. "Thank God, somebody's listening to me. Bayfield. Jonathan Bayfield. He's in room 403. He was admitted with a brain injury from a boxing match."

The nurse glanced over her shoulder at Arielle's parents, standing stock-still, their brows furrowed.

"Honey," Carey said. "Jonathan was admitted after you. You were both unconscious. You can't possibly know him."

"Is this a side effect of being in a coma?" Denise put before the nurse.

"Mother!" Arielle cringed. "My brain is just fine. Don't make this into something it's not. I just want to know how he is. Why can't anyone tell me?"

"Maybe you saw him on TV, or heard about one of his boxing matches?" the nurse suggested.

"No. No, I didn't."

"We're just trying to understand how you two could know each other," Carey explained. "Before the accident, you'd never been to California, and as far as I know from Coach, Jonathan has never been to Boston. Maybe your subconscious manufactured—"

Arielle cut him off. "I didn't manufacture anything. I'm not making this up." She searched their eyes. The gawking expression staring back at her made it perfectly clear she was on her own. "Fine, I'll go find out myself." She sat straight up and yanked off the monitor's wires, sending it into a frenzy.

Dr. Marcus entered at that moment with the lead nurse, halting the debate and Arielle's escape. "Dr. Yoo is in surgery, but I can take a look at Arielle." He offered her a rare, pleasant smile. "How are you feeling?" He flicked a pin light back and forth in her eyes.

She sighed. "Fine, but my parents think I'm one fry short of a Happy Meal."

"We certainly don't think that," Carey interjected.

Dr. Marcus swallowed back a chuckle, masking his humor. "Follow my finger."

Her eyes traveled the path of his finger several times with ease. "See? All good."

He reviewed her chart and nodded. "I like what I see."

"So, will you let me out of this bed?"

"I'd like to keep you on your IV and catheter a bit longer."

"Can't they come out now?"

Dr. Marcus arched a brow at her. "Some place you've got to be?"

She swallowed hard, her gaze darting between Dr. Marcus and her parents. He'd probably think she was delusional too, and it was absurdly apparent none of them would believe her if she told them the truth. Best to keep that one to herself. "I want to check on Jonathan—Jonathan Bayfield, and no one will tell me how he is."

His head jerked back slightly before he caught himself. He opened his mouth, but Denise didn't hesitate to sound off first. "She's got it in her head that she knows this boy."

Arielle groaned. "What am I, twelve? He's a man, mother, not a boy."

Her mother waved her away and faced Dr. Marcus. "I need your assurance that Arielle isn't suffering from some kind of altered perspective due to being in a coma."

"Again with the coma? Really, Mother?"

"Mrs. Robbins, Arielle is recovering nicely," he projected calmly. "I see no cause for alarm here." He glanced at Arielle. "In fact, I've changed my mind. I feel it may be good for her to get up and take a short walk. We'll first we need to remove your IV and catheter."

"Just do what you need to so I can check on Jonathan."

"Go ahead and remove her IV and catheter," Dr. Marcus instructed the nurse with the soft, soothing voice

"Yes, Dr. Marcus." She collected a few medical items, set them on a tray, and pulled the curtain around Arielle's bed for privacy. The IV slid right out, easing the stinging and swelling of her skin. The nurse replaced it with cotton gauze and a blue bandage before moving on to the catheter. As she pushed the bedding aside, she instructed, "Now blow out a large, deep breath."

Arielle inhaled as deep a breath as possible, then released it in one gust. A pinch of pressure burned inside her. Arielle twisted the blanket between her fingers. Seizing pain tugged at her pelvis as the catheter came free. "Oh my God. So not pleasant."

"It's all over," the nurse said, tucking Arielle back inside the covers. She opened the curtains and looked to Dr. Marcus. "Arielle's ready. Should I get a wheelchair?"

Arielle swung her legs over the side of the bed and protested, "I don't need a wheelchair."

Carey made a noise in his throat. "Arielle, you haven't been up and about for quite some time. It might be for the best to have the chair."

"I want to at least try on my own," she said, latching onto the bed railing and pushing to her feet.

Carey hovered next to her, his arms stretched out and ready. She held herself erect and let go of the railing. A smile of victory formed on her lips, but swiftly disappeared as her legs wobbled, then collapsed beneath her. Beads of sweat suddenly scattered across her forehead. "Wow, I feel super weak." She slumped forward, landing inside her father's arms.

"Not to worry, Arielle," Dr. Marcus ensured with a confident nod. "You'll gain your strength back very quickly now that you're awake."

"How about getting something to eat first before we go see Jonathan?" Carey encouraged, aiming her toward the bed.

Arielle resisted, leaning far away from the hospital bed. "I want to see him now. You're all freaking me out because no one will spill."

"Arielle, if you must see this boy —"

"Mother!"

"Very well," Denise conceded. "If you must see Jonathan, please let them bring you to him in a wheelchair."

"Yeah—okay," Arielle panted with uneven breaths.

"Let's get her a wheelchair," Dr. Marcus instructed the lead nurse, who briskly strode out the doorway and returned moments later, pushing a hospital color-coded wheelchair.

She lifted Arielle and deposited her onto the curved seat. "This will be much easier for you. We can work on walking later."

Carey intercepted the wheelchair and took hold of the handles. "I'll take it from here, thank you." He bowed in front of his daughter. "Your chariot awaits, my lady."

Arielle cracked a smile.

"Carey," Denise scoffed. "Arielle needs to rest. This isn't a game. Let's take her to see him and then get her back in bed." She then knelt in front of Arielle, plastering a grim expression on her face. "We didn't say anything because his condition is critical. You need to be prepared for what you're going to see. He's in a coma, hooked up to monitors like you were."

Arielle's lips parted, a small breath escaping before a heavy feeling sat in her stomach. "He should have awakened. Please, I need to see him."

"I need to check in on him, so I'll go as well." Dr. Marcus directed them into the hallway, leading the way.

The wheelchair rolled along the polished floor, the rubber wheels occasionally skidding in protest. Arielle's heartbeat throbbed inside her throat as the numbers 403 came into view.

Seconds later, Carey positioned her just outside the room and tapped the doorframe. "Hello, Coach, may we come in?"

Coach set the book he was reading aside and pushed to his feet. The young woman in a wheelchair blocking the doorway collided with his vision. He furrowed his brow and questioned, "Arielle?"

"She woke just a bit ago," Carey explained, "asking to see Jonathan."

Arielle's gaze shifted past Coach to Jonathan's still body, eyelids closed, head hidden behind a wall of bandages, but no ventilator. Her hands grew clammy and fear raced up her throat. He looked the same as the day Jekins brought her to his room, minus the awful hum of the ventilator. Thank God he was breathing on his own, but why hadn't he awakened? Her chin trembled, yet she held onto hope. There wasn't a reason to cry, not yet. "You promised me," she said aloud.

Coach glanced at Jonathan and back to Arielle. "You mean Jonathan? How could he prom..." His voice faded away.

Dr. Marcus inserted himself between Arielle and Coach. "Mr. Meyers, to your knowledge, does Jonathan know Arielle? Has he ever mentioned her?"

Coach slowly shook his head.

"We do know each other," Arielle assured.

Carey squeezed her shoulder. "We're going to get to the bottom of this confusion, honey."

She raised her voice. "There's no confusion. I know him, he knows me. I can't explain it, but it's true." She glanced back at Jonathan. "And he should be awake."

"Sometimes, coma patients go through a period of disorientation after waking," Dr. Marcus explained. "This could be what you're experiencing."

Impatience flushed across Arielle's cheeks as she released a breath of frustration before she spoke. "I'm not disoriented, or crazy, or whatever else everyone thinks." She aimed her attention at Coach. "I know you're Coach, his godparent, his guardian. You took him in after his parents died, the accident he feels responsible for. You helped him through that, got him into boxing." She paused to draw in a breath before continuing. "You like eighties rock music, and you play it for him because you think he likes it, but it only embarrasses him. He has the cutest dimples when he smiles, and he's so positive. I couldn't just make that stuff up."

Coach blinked several times before he openly stared. "How—how can you know any of that?"

"I told you, I know him—*really know him*." She exaggerated her words. "I'm not some creeper or stalker. I'm for real. Please, you've got to believe me."

Coach said nothing, a distant stare filling his eyes.

"Coach, can I please go to him?" Arielle begged.

He flapped his hand forward as if he had no control over it. "Yes, of course," he uttered.

"Thank you," she said, gripping the wheels and breaking free from her father's grasp, navigating to Jonathan's bedside. She took his hand in hers and pressed it to her cheek. "Come back to me, Jonathan. You promised." She waited for a sign, but none came. "It's okay." A sob hitched inside her chest. "I'll be right here when you wake."

"Okay, that's enough," Denise voiced in a challenging tone. "You need your rest. Let's get you back to your room."

"He needs me," Arielle gushed out. "I have to stay with him."

"He needs rest. You've seen him, now it's time to go." Denise whipped the wheelchair around and headed for the door.

Arielle craned her neck to keep Jonathan in view. "You don't under-stand. Something must have gone wrong; otherwise, he would've woken up. He wouldn't do this to me."

Denise quickened her pace. "You're not making any sense, and you need to rest."

Adrenaline sprang Arielle to her feet, and she leapt from the chair to Jonathan's bed, climbing up next to him and flinging her arms about him. She clung to him, crying, "Please, I have to stay."

Denise's mouth gaped before she snapped it shut. "This is ridicu-lous." She yanked on Arielle's arm, trying to peel her off of Jonathan. "You're acting like a child. Get down from there, now!"

"You treat me like a child," Arielle fired back. "Always telling me what to do. You've never once showed faith in me. Never once allowed me to make my own choices." She threw a leveled glare at her mother. "Now, I'm telling *you*, I'm staying."

"Denise," Carey finally spoke up. "Let it go."

Dr. Marcus brushed his shoe across the floor, keeping his gaze lowered. Family drama was not his forte.

Coach eyed Arielle with sympathy, then shifted his focus to Jonathan. He'd kept a lovely, peaceful atmosphere in his room, and all this yelling wasn't helping anyone, especially Jonathan.

He rested a hand on Denise's shoulder and spoke in a calm, soft voice. "Denise, it's all right. Arielle's welcome to stay. There's no need to argue."

She turned sharply, staring down Coach. "I will not have my daughter acting like a—"

"Arielle?" Bayfield moaned out in a hoarse whisper.

Arielle jerked her head toward his voice. "Jonathan?" His eyes peered up into hers. Tears spilled over her eyelids, falling onto his cheeks. "I'm here," she said before smothering his face with kisses.

"Jonathan!" Coach cried, rushing to his bedside and latching onto his hand, giving it a heartfelt squeeze. "Thank God."

Dr. Marcus pushed his way through Arielle's parents, then Coach, to get to Bayfield's bedside. "Arielle, I need to take a look at him."

Arielle clung to him, not budging an inch.

Bayfield tucked a lock of her hair behind her ear. "It's okay, Arielle."

"You scared me."

He softly kissed her lips and murmured, "You're stuck with me, remember? I'm not going anywhere."

"Promise?"

"I promise."

Arielle scooted to the side of the bed, giving Dr. Marcus enough breathing room to examine him.

Bayfield's gaze landed on Coach, and he returned the squeeze of Coach's hand.

Coach's chin quivered. "You scared me too, buddy."

He felt tears welling and blinked them away. "Never meant to worry you. I'm feeling much better now."

"I can substantiate that," Dr. Marcus agreed. "Your vital signs are looking good."

Bayfield brushed a hand over the puckered cloth covering his head. "When can I lose the bandage?"

"We can discuss that later. Right now, I'm going leave you alone so you can visit with your family. I'll stop back in while to check on you."

Coach gripped the doctor's hand. "Thank you, Dr. Marcus."

He returned Coach's handshake. "You're most welcome." He gave the group his customary nod before exiting the room.

All eyes turned to Arielle and Bayfield. Coach beamed. "There are no words to express how relieved and elated I am that you're okay, both of you."

"Yes." Carey breathed a sigh of relief.

A shiver of relief prickled Denise's spine as she reached for the strength of Carey's hand. "We were all so worried." Her voice grew faint, losing its domination. "I'm grateful my daughter is awake and healthy." She looked to Coach. "I'm very happy for you and your son as well." She let go of Carey's hand to sink onto the bench along the wall. "This has been an emotional time for us all. Thank God you're both out of the woods."

"Yes," Coach joyfully agreed. A frown settled into his forehead, annihilating the glee. He shifted his focus to Arielle and Jonathan cuddled together in the bed. "What's puzzling is how the two of you know each other, and quite well I might add."

"We're curious about that as well," Carey seconded Coach's sentiments.

Bayfield and Arielle stole a look, conveying the secret knowledge they shared between them. Bayfield brushed off their concern with a weak flap of his hand. "How we met isn't relevant. We want to be together. That's all that matters."

Arielle echoed Bayfield feelings. "Jonathan's my soulmate."

Bayfield smirked. "Literally."

"Yes. I couldn't image my life without him."

Coach reacted with a slow, disbelieving shake of his head. Carey became suddenly still, and Denise pressed her hand against her chest, splaying her fingers. Coach found his voice first.

"Jonathan, I'll admit I'm at a loss, and truly don't know how to react, but your happiness is what matters most in my world." Coach gripped Jonathan's hand, then Arielle's, squeezing both between his palms. "If you're happy, then I'm happy. I love you, buddy."

Jonathan's eyes grew glassy. "I love you too, Coach."

Carey came around to Arielle's side, bent over, and kissed the top of her head. "Honey, I can't begin to understand how this came about. You're my world, and I love you to the moon and back. I'm with Coach. If you're happy, I'm happy."

Arielle reached up and kissed his cheek. "I love you too, Dad."

A bark of laughter flew out of Denise's mouth. "How can the two of you be okay with this? It makes no sense." She wagged a finger their way. "A month ago, I'm quite certain neither of you had knowledge of other. Now, you can't live with each other. I don't agree with your father or Coach. This is some sort of fantasy. If you want my blessing, you'll have to prove to me that what you say you feel is real and over a steady length of time.

Arielle beamed and held her chin high. "I will. I'll prove it to you, Mother."

Chapter 25

A bolt of lightning streaked across the living room, shadowed by a series of booming blasts, blocking Sull from reaching the front door. The bursts, mimicking gunfire, ricocheted off the walls and lit up the room like the fourth of July. He dove behind the sofa, shouting over the noise, "Jekins, take cover!"

Jekins stooped over, dodging flashes of light whizzing through the air, and hightailing it to the sofa. "What the hell's going on?"

"The book..." A knot of fear constricted Sull's throat, silencing him.

"Don't freak out on me now, Father!" Jekins smacked him between the shoulder blades, dislodging the lump.

Sull coughed up the remnants of his fright before his voice returned. "We must not have defeated it." He peered around the sofa's edge at an array of colors swirling inside the lightstorm and lighting up his living room. "I'm certain we didn't."

Jekins inched his head over the back of the sofa and ducked back down. "That life-size kaleidoscope is heading our way."

Sull nodded, a glazed look in his eyes. "Yes, it would seem so."

Jekins stiffened. "What, no prayer to get us through this one, Father?"

A splitting sound, like fabric ripping apart, whooshed across the ceiling. A gaping hole emerged, shedding unnatural beams of glaring light and calling forth a rage of rumbling thunder. Another strike shook the foundation—the universe seemingly cracking wide open.

Sull gripped Jekins's hand. "Heavenly Father, uphold us and keep us safe from the evil that encircles us. Put Your hedge of protection and safety around us and place a guard at our doors."

Howling gusts of wind drowned out Sull's voice as the heart of the storm corkscrewed with a powerful vengeance. A brilliant white flame swiftly appeared and sparkled in the center of the room, as if the hand of God had reached down and swept the wickedness into a vacuum, before spreading a dead calm zone over the room.

Sull and Jekins glanced at each before slowly rising and peering over the sofa. Drara's lifeless body, curled into a fetal position, laid in the center of the living room.

"Drara," Jekins gasped, racing toward her. He crumpled to his knees, his hands fluttering about her, afraid to touch her. "She's not moving!" His eyes roamed quickly over her armor—the tarnished metal replaced by sparkling silver. "Jesus."

Jekins's shrill voice set Sull in motion. He skidded to a stop in front of Drara. "Look at her veins, they're white!"

Jekins clutched his arms to his chest. "Is she dead?"

Sull observed the mystical creature. Her anatomy was completely foreign to him. How did one check the vitals of a being not of this earth? He glanced at Jekins's grief-stricken face. He had to do something and did the only thing he knew to do. Sull bent over her, placing his ear on her chest. A steady thump echoed against his eardrum. He jerked upright and shouted, "She's got a heartbeat. She's alive!"

Jekins's shoulders caved as a shudder of relief ran through him. Sull's words gave him the strength he needed to finally touch her, and he brushed a loose dreadlock off her forehead and tucked it behind her ear.

Drara gasped out loud before her eyelids flew open. She sat straight up, her eyes darting about the room.

Jekins blinked, and then gazed into a pair of blue eyes. He shook his head and did a double take. He hadn't imagined it; Drara's eyes were definitely blue—ice blue to be precise. He gently reached out his hand. "Drara, it's me, Jekins."

She held him in view, her newly colored orbs constricting. "Jekins?"

Shaky laughter spilled from his lips. "Yes."

She shifted her gaze to Sull, then back to Jekins, splaying her fingers over her chest. "I am alive." Her gaze caught a flash of silver. She slowly looked over her body, then held out her arms, blinking at the white veins running through her flesh. The skeleton necklace she'd worn around her neck for countless years was gone. "What has happened to me?"

Sull offered her his hand and lifted her to her feet. "You destroyed the book, Drara. Ridded the world of its evil. You're a savior to those souls."

Jekins stood by her side, a proud grin on his face. "These are your true colors, Drara." He glanced about the room. A framed mirror sat above the fireplace, and he ushered Drara in front of it. "Look."

Drara's eyelashes fluttered before her reflection. Her armor, tailored into a gallant Knight's sparkling silver, gleamed with pride. The cat-like yellowish orbs she had been plagued with transformed into a fairy-tale blue, and her once hideous colorless lips spread into a lovely rosy-pink smile. Drara cupped her hands over cheeks as soft laughter flowed out of her.

"Human, I am almost beautiful."

Jekins wrapped an arm around her and gave her shoulder a squeeze. "You *are* beautiful, Drara."

Chapter 26

Bayfield glanced at Arielle snuggled next to him in his hospital bed, before setting his sights on the various rooftops peeking through the room's large bay window. "I had no idea hospitals had private rooms like these."

Arielle kissed his cheek. "Of course they do. Slebs would get mobbed if they had rooms in the regular part of the hospital. This floor keeps the famous people's personal business personal."

"Is that why your parents insisted on us sharing a private room? To keep the whole mess quiet?"

"Probably."

He eyed the empty bed next to his. "Not that you're ever in your bed."

"Seriously? You want me over there?"

He laughed out loud and planted a big smooch on her lips. His lips lingered on hers as he gazed into her beautiful brown eyes. "I want you with me, always."

"Perfect answer." She settled back against the pillow, a content smile spreading on her lips. "And it's finally nice to have the room to ourselves. I didn't think my parents and Coach would ever leave."

He thrust a fist in the air. "Hunger triumphed. Enjoy it while it lasts. They'll be back from dinner soon, and the third degree will resume."

Arielle faced him. "I have a question of my own."

He caught the uncertainty in her tone and pulled her close. "What is it?"

"Do you think she made it?"

"Who, Drara?"

She bit her lip and nodded.

His gaze drifted toward the ceiling. "I hope so. I thought there'd be a connection or something, you know, because of the whole anchor thing. But I feel nothing, not even a flicker of her, like the whole thing never happened."

Arielle cupped his chin and turned his head toward her. "I did too, and to tell you the truth, I'm glad the whole thing is over, connection or not."

A slight grimace formed on his brow. "We helped her destroy the book. I don't get why everything just ended." He swallowed hard. "Unless she didn't make it."

Arielle sat upright and pulled her knees into her chest. "That freaks me out. I mean, can she really be dead?"

He laced his fingers between hers, giving them a squeeze. "I don't really know, but I hope she's alive." He looked out the window as he revealed, "She did something for me—something I'll never forget." His eyes found hers. "And the reason why I didn't wake when you did."

"Tell me."

"That weird place, where we landed, and Drara let go of you?"

"Yes?"

His chin quivered and he sucked in a breath. "She held me back because of my parents." He squeezed his eyelids shut. "I know this is going to sound crazy..."

"Really? After everything we've been through, I'm pretty sure I'm gonna believe you."

Bayfield looked at her with wet eyes. "It was my parents. They brought us to that place. Drara knew. Somehow, she knew to let go of you so they would come forward. I tried to follow you, but Drara hung onto me. Because of her, I got to see my parents, hear their voices. They said the accident wasn't my fault." Tears rolled down his cheeks. "That they were proud of me, for me to be happy and to live my life."

Arielle brushed away his tears and kissed him softly. She held him in her arms and whispered, "I believe every word."

A knock and a clearing of a throat pulled Bayfield and Arielle apart, shifting their gazes toward the doorway and on Sull. "May I come in?"

Arielle scooted off the bed and greeted him with a big hug. "Of course."

Bayfield gingerly climbed out of bed, slowly inching across the floor. He extended his hand.

"Hey, Father."

Sull squeezed Bayfield's hand in return. "How are you both? When I didn't see you in ICU, I thought the worst. One of the nurses must have seen the panic on my face and put me out of my misery by giving me your new room number." He looked around the room, nodding. "Not bad...not bad at all."

"Arielle's father has connections." Bayfield grinned at her. "We have him to thank for this room."

"My dad's money can be very persuasive."

Sull's gaze circled back to Bayfield and Arielle, and he again asked, "Really, how are you both?"

Arielle slipped her arm through Bayfield's. "I'm almost back to normal. Jonathan's healing a little slower, but his injury was much worse."

"I'm doing okay." Bayfield offered a confident nod, then frowned. "Though, I'm hobbling around like an old man who gets tired real fast."

Sull plastered a serious expression on his face as he laid a hand of each of their shoulders. "You've been through a harrowing and appalling journey. I've asked the Lord for his strength, and for a swift recovery for you both."

Arielle snuggled closer to Bayfield and gazed into his eyes. "I think we're gonna be just fine."

"I'd go through it all over again just to meet her."

She looked up at him and smiled. "I would too."

Sull offered them a thoughtful expression. "I'm glad you both found happiness out of such darkness."

Bayfield looked away from Arielle to acknowledge Sull. "Thank you, Father."

"Yes, thank you," Arielle echoed.

"Is there anything I can do for the two of you?" Sull asked.

Bayfield shared a look with Arielle, his desire to learn Drara's fate etched across his brow. Arielle gave him a hesitant nod.

With determination thick in his voice, Bayfield asked, "How is Drara?" He wagged a finger at himself, then at Arielle. "We're both freaking out about whether she made it or not. I'm taking that you haven't said otherwise is a good sign, but we need you to say it."

Sull grinned. "She did indeed make it."

Bayfield rushed out an authoritative, "I want to see her!"

"I can arrange that."

Chapter 27

Jekins let the BMW idle inside the motor court of Drara's palace. The night's starlit backdrop fell over the property, casting an angelic glow. The massive structure, once bustling with numerous souls, stood dark, empty, and devoid of life. Jekins regarded Drara, sitting quietly in the passenger's seat, hands folded neatly in her lap, gaze locked on the mansion's front door. He gave it his best effort to remain silent, but his sentiments got the better of him. "Are you sure you have to burn the place down? Can't you just remove your magic from its walls?"

Drara's orbs shifted from the palace to Jekins. "What if I miss a room or two, and some poor human steps into a pocket of that overlooked magic? Their body would be turned inside outside and ripped apart. What then?"

Jekins held a hand up, warding off the commentary. "Okay, okay, I get it...but fire? What if it spreads, endangering the surrounding area?"

She deliberately raised her eyebrows and presented him with a look that radiated superiority. "It is magical fire, Jekins. It burns only what I command of it, nothing more."

He didn't let up. "It's just such a shame. We're going to sit back and watch millions of dollars go up in smoke."

She waved a dismissive hand his way. "There's no need to concern yourself over finances. I have plenty of money."

"Do I even want to know how that's possible?"

"It is nothing sinister or corrupt. My past humans left it to me."

Jekins's shoulders drooped before he could catch his emotions. "I see."

Her eyes softened. "None have meant to me what you do." She hesitantly rested her hand on his. "You are my family, Jekins. I care for you."

He enfolded her hand between his and beheld her with warm devotion. "I am quite fond of you as well. I wish I had something of monetary value I could leave you when it's my time."

She traced the white veins running through her translucent hand lying against his porcelain skin. He had always accepted her, never once making her feel abnormal or inhuman. She met his kind eyes. "Your friendship is what I cherish most. What if you did not have to die? What if I could give you immortality?"

Jekins jerked his head back, then shook it. "What? That's impossible."

Drara's heart fluttered inside her armor. She quickly withdrew her hand and pressed it over her chest, quieting the trepidation. "It is possible, dear human. My magic will grant you eternal life."

Jekins held his hands up in a defensive stance. "Pretty sure that's breaking the laws of nature, not to mention the universe."

"My magic has never been more powerful than it is now." She cocked her head and reconsidered her words. "However, I may only use my gift for noble acts."

"I hardly call giving me immortality noble."

"I disagree. It prevents both of us from experiencing the sorrow of parting."

Jekins leaned away from Drara, making a tsking sound. "I don't know, Drara. Living forever sounds more like dark magic than good magic. Are you sure you've got this right?"

She blinked, then offered him a slow, disbelieving shake of her head. "Do you not want to stay with me?"

A kind expression spread across Jekins's face as he reached for her hand. "Of course I do. I've been with you for forty years. You're like a daughter to me, Drara, but how is this even possible? Thousands of things could go wrong."

"No," she insisted. "The magic that lives inside me, that flows through my veins, is omnipotent, incapable of doing harm, only good. I cannot explain it, only that my body and mind know it to be true."

Jekins heaved a sigh as if to surrender, then inquired, "So how would this work?"

Drara stared at him, her pupils dilating. She struggled to find the right words, yet there wasn't a subtle way to enlighten him. In her superior and composed manner, she put before him, "As I stated, my magic has the power to grant eternal life. It flows through my blood, and I must offer it to you."

A sudden coldness hit Jekins's core. He ducked his chin to hide his neck as his eyes bulged out of their sockets. "That sounds a little too vampiric for my taste."

Drara swatted at the air and tossed a scowl his way. "Nonsense. A being such as myself cannot be compared to a bloodsucking myth!"

"What am I to compare it to, Drara?" he demanded, his voice raising to a shrill pitch. "For the first nineteen years of my life, I had no idea a being such as yourself existed." He held up a hand, warding off the remark he perceived was on its way. "Yes, being psychic made me privy to the unexplainable, but I witnessed human spirits, not unearthly creatures." He placed his head in his hands, inhaling and exhaling several deep, calming breaths before facing her. "This thing you're talking about, have you ever done it before?"

Drara slanted her body away from Jekins as her eyes widened in disbelief. "I would never allow harm to come to you. If there were any possibilities of danger, I would never have mentioned it." Her voice lost its poise as she admitted, "However, no, I have never performed such a spell, nor have I wanted to, until now—until you."

An intense glow burned inside Jekins's eyes as he absorbed the meaning behind her words. Would he still be human or become like her, invisible to the many? Would he gain supernatural powers, gifts, strengths? Would he condemn himself to a life of doom if he accepted? Did he want such a life? It was foreign to everything he knew. Could he even consider immortality? Yet the possibility of it nagged at his brain.

Drara clasped her fingers, pressing them into the nervous flutter of her stomach. She'd been isolated, alone, walking the human earth for an immeasurable lifetime until she met Jekins. Her mind flew back, throwing her in front of a nineteen-year-old boy who looked upon her without fear then and now. He had welcomed her into his life, a life she now treasured. Yet, whatever his decision, she must respect it, regardless of her own wishes. A shudder passed through her as she longed with every ounce of her being his acceptance of her offer.

Jekins spoke, breaking the silence, "Would I remain a human or—"

"I cannot change one lifeform into another. My blood suspends the aging process. You would not grow another day older, and your body would become immune to sickness and disease."

"So, no special powers? I won't become invisible? Nothing like that?"

She presented him with a puzzled look. "Why would you assume this?"

He deliberately lowered his head to stare at her. "Oh, I don't know, maybe because the magic flowing inside you, you're handing off to me."

"It is not like that."

"Then what's it like, Drara? Tell me."

"I cannot turn you into something you are not. You are human. You will stay human. The *only* thing that will change is that you will not age. Everything else will remain as it is now."

Jekins held up his hands in an apologetic manner. "I'm sorry. It's just...I don't understand any of this. I'm at a loss."

"Yes, you are right, it is a lot to take in." Her expression softened. "It is I who should apologize."

He swallowed several times, attempting to rid himself of the lump sitting in his throat. "How exactly would I receive your blood?"

Drara reached for his hand. Turning over his palm and tracing a finger over his lifeline, she said, "I slice open your lifeline, then mine, spilling our blood." She pressed his palm against hers. "Our hands are joined, and as our lifeblood merges, I recite a bonding spell." She pulled her hand away. "Then it is done."

He stared at his open palm and let out a quick laugh. "Sounds simple."

She shrugged. "As you humans say, a piece of cake."

He pursed his lips. "Can I think about it?"

"Of course." Her stomach clenched, and she broke eye contact. Hopelessness spread through her, wilting her shoulders. "I must take care of the palace." Drara scurried out of the car before Jekins could see the disappointment moistening her eyes. The despair, the torment, and rejection fueled her magic. She charged forward, arms spread, hands rigid, and aimed at her palace. She slapped her hands together, sparking bright orange flames. A sizzling hiss leapt into firebombs twirling inside her palms. "With these flames, I purge each palace wall. Burn one, burn all. Thy ashes must fall."

She hurled her weapons of fire into the air, striking the center of the palace. The structure ignited. A light show of orange, yellow, and red flames danced across the surface in absolute silence. Jekins stumbled out of the car, mouth gaping, eyes widened and transfixed on the palace.

He steadied himself before standing by her side. "Jesus," he uttered. "How is it not making a sound?"

"It is magical fire," Drara reminded him. "It is like ants carrying away crumbs at a picnic."

He jerked his head toward her. "What?"

"My magic is caving in on itself, piece by piece." She glanced toward her masterpiece, admiring the array of colors flickering inside the blaze. "Soon my palace will collapse and crumble, its ashes vanishing into the wind." Drara gestured toward the car. "Come, human, there are six more houses I must burn."

Jekins slapped his hands against his cheeks. "Jesus. Six?"

With a slow, steady gait, Drara approached Jekins and looped her arm through his, guiding him toward the car. "Yes. You were not my first human, remember? There are my homes from my previous humans that we must also burn."

Chapter 28

Arielle and Bayfield claimed one of Cliff Park's highly sought-after benches, facing the ocean's horizon, with its serenading waves crashing below. The park was home to cyclists, skateboarders, joggers, and hikers, seeking the challenge of its many trails, whereas photographers flocked to its panoramic ocean views, hoping to snap that award-winning shot.

Arielle gazed upon the rainbow sunset peeking through the park's lofty trees as the constant whir of wheels skating across the park's walkways sounded off in the background. She slipped her hand inside Bayfield's jacket pocket and glanced away from the sherbet-colored sky to look into his eyes. "The sunset is absolutely beautiful."

He kissed her lips softly. "You're beautiful. I've never seen anyone as beautiful as you."

A blissful smile brightened her face, then she laughed. "That's so sappy." She kissed him back. "But I love it, and I love you."

"I love you too." He squeezed her tight, his face beaming. "I don't think I've ever been this happy."

"Me either." She stomped her boots on the cement. "And it feels so good!"

He tilted his head toward the sky, a content sigh escaping him as the sunlight reflected on the scar cutting through his hairline.

Arielle traced a finger along the bubbled incision. "Your hair's growing back."

He brushed a hand over his hair, tugging it forward. "Finally."

"The scar's sexy. Don't hide it."

"What did I do to deserve you?"

"I could say the same about you."

He burst out laughing. "We're both totally whipped."

Giving him a playful nudge, she replied with, "No, we're in love."

He settled back against the bench, one arm hooked about its back, the other around Arielle. "This is a strange place to meet Drara. So many people. You'd think they'd want a place more—I don't know—private."

"Well, she's bailed twice now. Maybe Jekins thought a crowded place would work better, but who knows?"

He furrowed his brow. "I think she's nervous."

"About seeing us?"

"Not sure. It's just the vibe I've been getting ever since I asked to see her."

"Maybe she's done with the whole mess and just wants to be left alone, like she's flipped an off switch or something." She waved the statement away. "Or maybe it's guilt for everyone at the palace. Who knows what happened to all those poor people." She shuddered at the thought.

Bayfield rubbed her arms as he reassured, "I'm sure everyone woke as we did—some probably not too happy about it."

"I guess. But I still feel we should have warned them."

"Sometimes not knowing is better than knowing," he conveyed. "I thought about it, and if we'd gone back there and told everyone that the party was coming to an end, I think they would've freaked."

"I don't know. Maybe." Arielle laid her hand over her heart. "At least I know Sara found peace."

A distant stare claimed Bayfield as his brain pressed play, conjuring up Sara crossing the threshold. "Yes, she did."

Before the sorrow over Sara's death could claim her, Arielle steered the conversation back to Drara. "What time's the meetup with Catwoman and her wingmen?"

He scowled playfully at her. "Really, still?"

She shrugged and blew him a kiss.

"At 6:30, and it's 6:45. They're late."

"God, I hope she doesn't back out again."

Bayfield glanced over his shoulder, surveying the walkway. "I just wanted to thank her, but if she doesn't show this time, I'm done."

Arielle hugged him. "I know."

He buried his head in her embrace, losing himself in the scent of her skin, and diverting his thoughts away from Drara.

Arielle caught sight of Sull hiking up the pathway. She raised her hand, catching his attention. In Bayfield's ear, she whispered, "Sull is coming over."

Bayfield's head jerked upright, his gaze darting over his shoulder and landing on the Father. Jekins and Drara were MIA. Tension spread through his face as he groaned, "Figures."

Sull reached the bench, and Arielle popped up and greeted him with a warm hug. "So good to see you, Father."

He patted her on the back and gave a crisp nod. "And you, Arielle." He released her and offered his hand to Bayfield. "You look good, Jonathan."

Bayfield got to his feet and squeezed Sull's hand. "Thank you." He gestured to his head, then swiped a hand across the incision. "Pretty much all back to normal, except for this scar."

"Barely noticeable."

"It adds to his character," Arielle chimed in, locking arms with Bayfield.

Bayfield leaned over and kissed her cheek before shifting his gaze back to the walkway. "She's not coming, is she?"

"Jekins and Drara will be here. We thought it best if I arrived beforehand." He pursed his lips. "Drara's changed. Destroying the book has had a profound effect on her."

"Changed how?"

Sull weighed his words. "Let's just say, her appearance is...well, rather angelic, and her nature far less superior."

"What?" Arielle blurted out. "No more Catwoman?"

Bayfield cocked his head as he repeated, "Angelic?"

Sull rolled his hand in a circular fashion and rattled off one of his theories. "There's a part of me that wants to believe the universe pays it forward—you protect it, it rewards you. In a sense, Drara prevented an evil apocalypse. I believe this was the universe's way of rewarding her."

"Reward?" Arielle flapped a hand, dismissing the idea. "She started the whole mess."

"In all fairness, the book started it," Bayfield professed, defending Drara. "She was just one of its victims."

Arielle huffed and waved the remark away. "A victim that kept the whole *Alice in Wonderland* thing going."

"Drara's intentions in the start may have been selfish," Sull pointed out, "but in the end, she did the right thing."

"I'll give her that," Arielle acknowledged half-heartedly.

Bayfield rushed out his words like a kid on Christmas morning. "When will they get here? I want to see her."

"Jekins will text me when they arrive." Sull pulled out his cell, swiping the screen.

"Nothing yet."

"They're not coming." Bayfield's words no sooner flowed from his mouth when a chime came from Sull's cell.

He checked his messages and presented Bayfield with a thumbs-up. "They're here."

Bayfield reached for Arielle's hand, and she clasped his with a reassuring squeeze. "Are you nervous?"

Bayfield was overthinking it. It was just a meeting, and with a creature he barely knew. He just wanted to thank her, show his appreciation. His parents would want that, expect that. Bayfield flinched his head back slightly and gathered his brows. Was that what this was all about, his parents? His gaze drifted upward, past the clouds, searching the darkening blue sky, remembering his mother's words that she was watching over him from above. Warmth spread through his chest and his eyes watered. All of this was for her, not Drara. Soft laughter spilled from his lips. He wiped his eyes and hugged Arielle. "No, I'm not nervous. My mother would want me to thank Drara. I'm doing this for her."

Arielle squeezed him tight, her own eyes prickling with tears. "I get it. I'll be right by your side."

Sull touched Bayfield's shoulder. "They're here."

Bayfield turned around with eyes wide, searching. They found Drara, an arm's length away from him, standing at Jekins's side, adorned by silver armor.

Drara's ice blue eyes darted about before centering on Bayfield and Arielle. "Hello, Jonathan, Arielle." Her rose pink lips offered a polite, and slightly apologetic smile.

Bayfield squeezed out a high-pitched, "Hello."

Arielle stood completely still, mouth slacken, then clutched her stomach. "Oh my God, Drara!" She approached her with a hand stretched out in front of her. "Wow...I mean, this is crazy. You're like X-Men's Storm."

Drara looked at her questioningly. "Is that a good thing?"

Arielle slapped her forehead. "Uh, yeah. She's, like, a superhero."

A satisfied smirk claimed Drara's lips. "Thank you." She side-stepped past Arielle and confronted Bayfield. Her gaze narrowed as she locked her orbs on his. "I heard you wanted to see me."

Bayfield blinked rapidly, taking in the new Drara. Her ivory-colored veins twisting beneath sparkling silver armor, and the brilliance of her ice blue eyes did resemble a version of Storm, but more angelic as Sull had stated. The skeleton key and the book, no longer a part of her gear, but it was her rose pink lips he couldn't get past. They were so... human-like. "Y—Yes." The word stumbled over his tongue. "I did."

Jekins scooted by Arielle, making his way toward Sull.

Arielle did a double take. "Wow, Jekins, skinny jeans and a sweater? What happened to the tux and top hat?"

Jekins took a bow. "My chauffeur days are over, Miss Robbins. I have retired, as you referred to it, my 'Mad Hatter' look."

She gave him a playful nudge. "This look is much cooler."

"Why thank you." He gave her a kind nod and proceeded on his way. He claimed a spot next to Sull. "Father."

Sull briefly took his eyes off Bayfield and acknowledged, "Jekins."

Bayfield openly stared at Drara, losing his train of thought. "Um, I wanted to...you look so different."

An inner glow brightened Drara's eyes. "I am different."

Bayfield gave his head a good shake, clearing his thoughts. "Sorry, I don't mean to stare." He pushed his shoulders back and stood tall. "I wanted to see you so I could thank you. What you did, letting me see my parents, is something I'll never forget." He took her hand in his.

Drara cocked her head and eyed him with an unfocused gaze. "My actions were logical. Gratitude is not necessary."

"For me, it's especially necessary." He laid his hand on his heart, then gestured toward Drara. "I need to do this, so please, let me thank you," he told her, his voice thick with emotion.

She dipped her chin in acknowledgement.

"Thank you, Drara, for giving me one more moment with my parents."

"You are most welcome."

Arielle brushed a tear from her cheek and squeezed Jonathan's hand.

Observing from afar, Jekins leaned closer to Sull and offered up, "My speculations were correct."

Sull folded his arms and gave Jekins a sidelong glance. "What speculations?"

Jekins lifted a palm, aiming it toward Bayfield, Arielle, and Drara. "Jonathan's request to see Drara got me thinking. Their souls are tucked safely inside their bodies. Technically, they shouldn't be able to see her anymore." He pursed his lips. "Them not being psychic and all."

Sull's hands dropped to his sides. "I hadn't thought of that."

"Clearly, they see each other."

"Clearly."

"I chose this location for its crowds," Jekins explained. "Drara's been moping about the house, rambling on about making me immortal."

Sull jerked his head, then formed the sign of the cross over Jekins.

Jekins pushed his hand away. "Don't go all priestly on me. I didn't agree, which is her dilemma. She's terrified of being alone once I'm gone." He pointed at her. "I thought if they could see her, then others may as well, so..."

Sull grinned and finished his sentence. "So, you brought her here to see if it sparks a reaction from a passerby or two."

Jekins gave a joyful nod. "That I did. She is undoubtedly catching the fancy of the public, though she hasn't caught on yet." He nudged the Father's shoulder. "Take a gander."

Sull spotted a cyclist whizzing down the pathway. He homed in on the man just as he passed Drara. There was a slight twist of his head to look at her before speeding on by. Sull slapped his thigh. "Ha! You're right." A frown appeared, gathering his brows. "How is Drara not catching this?"

Jekins shrugged. "Not sure."

The smallest voice cut in on their conversation. "Mommy, look! An angel."

Jekins and Sull turned, following the voice. A child, not more than five or six, ran along the trail with her arms stretched wide, rushing toward Drara, her mother hurrying after her. As the child reached Drara, she flung her arms around her, tilting her head upward, face beaming at Drara. "Hi," the child squealed.

Drara's mouth fell open as she gawked at the tiny human clinging to her legs.

Arielle and Bayfield stumbled into each other, hands flying to their mouths.

Jekins and Sull rushed over, reaching Drara at the same time the mother pried her child off Drara and scooped her into her arms.

"I'm so sorry," the mother said. "She's too young to understand the meaning of a costume."

Sull swooped in front of the stunned Drara. "No apology needed. Have a lovely evening."

"You as well," the mother said, carrying her child away.

The child looked over her mother's shoulder and waved at Drara. "Bye-bye, pretty angel."

"What the hell?" Bayfield finally got out. "Other people can see you now?"

Arielle frowned. "Wait a minute..." Her gaze darted from Drara to Bayfield, and back to Drara. "We"—she pointed at herself and Bayfield—"shouldn't be able to see her now either. How is this happening?"

Bayfield blinked. "That's right, we're complete, the whole mess behind us. How can we...? What the hell's going on?"

Drara opened her mouth, yet she didn't speak a word.

"I had a hunch," Jekins offered up, "but had to test it out." He spread his arms wide. "And what do you know, I was right!"

A skateboarder approached at high speed, the wheels humming along the cement as he zigzagged between Drara and Bayfield. "That's some sick armor, girlie!" he yelled over his shoulder as his board whisked him down the pathway.

Drara shuffled back and into Jekins. He wrapped an arm around her, steadying her. She looked up into his eyes, shaking her head and voicing denial. "No, it can't be. Are people able to see me?" She glanced down at her hands, turning them palm side up. "Am I visible?"

Jekins kissed the top of her head. "It appears very much so."

Sull bobbed his head and shouted out, "What did I tell you? The universe pays it forward!"

Bayfield sank onto the bench and pulled Arielle down with him. "Jesus."

Arielle snuggled inside his jacket, wrapping her arms around him. "Drara's visible now? How's that possible?"

"We may never know the how, but believe it, folks, something good came out of all of this." Jekins placed his hands on Drara's shoulders and looked her in the eyes. "You'll never be alone ever again. You don't need me. The whole world is at your fingertips now."

A kind smile danced in her eyes. "Then I shall cherish every moment we have together, dear human. But my offer will remain if you should ever change your mind."

Jekins gave her a nod and a warm smile.

Arielle shook her head in disbelief. "This is totally nutso."

"Yeah," Bayfield agreed, narrowing his gaze on Drara. Was Sull right? Had the universe paid it forward? Deep in thought, his gaze roamed upward, catching sight of the stars making their appearance in the darkening sky. The twinkling lights triggered the memory of his parents, and the many souls floating about inside that dark dome. His parents had been there for him, but why the others, and why so many? What was their purpose? As questions spun around his brain, again he eyed Drara. Squeezing Arielle's knee, he said, "I'm gonna talk Drara for a minute."

"Okay."

Bayfield pulled Drara aside. "Can I talk to you for a minute?"

"You may."

Hands in his pockets, he rocked back and forth on his heels. "What happened after you let go of me? Why were all those souls there? What did they want?"

"I want to..." She frowned. "I believe the phrase is 'get it off my chest.'" She locked her eyes on his. "Your parents restrained me, interlocking their arms about my body as they called to the many souls. Hundreds surrounded me, their bright light encircling me, confining my movements. I feared they had come to harm me, to punish me for the book. Though, I did not want to die, I accepted my fate and declared, 'I am prepared to die.' Your mother's eyes held inside of them a kindness I have never known. Then she spoke." Drara paused and released a shallow breath.

"Come on. What did she say?"

"That I was not there to die, but to gain a soul. I stood still, thinking I misheard her, then flashes of light blinded me. I had to shield my eyes and look away, though I felt them, all of them, laying their hands on me and piercing my armor. One by one, they began to retreat, yet your parents stayed behind, their hands joined with mine. Your mother stared at me for some time, her eyes moist with tears, and then blurted out, "Thank you for saving my son." They vanished with the others to some place outside of the dome, leaving me alone."

Bayfield swallowed a thick sob rising in his throat.

Drara gave him a moment before continuing. "I began to search for a way out when a strange bolt of lightning crackled inside of the dome, striking me. The next time I opened my eyes, I was lying on the Father's floor."

Bayfield gawked at her, his brain trying to form words, but nothing came. If he hadn't gone through everything he had, he would've blown off Drara's statement. That kind of shit just didn't happen. But it had happened. He'd lived it. "That's bat-shit crazy, Drara. So, like, are you human now?"

"I am..." Her voice faded with uncertainty before finding its power. "I am still a mystical being, yet now blessed with a soul."

He eyed her, this creature his parents chose to save, who had saved him and all the others who had signed that jacked-up book. "My parents saw the good in people, all people. I think they saw the good in you too. In my book, that says a lot." He stuck out his hand. "Friends?"

She stared at his open palm before meeting his eyes. He smiled at her. He had his mother's smile. Drara placed her hand inside his. "Friends."

About The Author

LAURA DALEO is the author of five books. She is best known for her storytelling of the vampiric persuasion. Her most recent work, The Vampire Within, is the third book in her Immortal Kiss series. The series is an interesting twist on the Egyptian pantheon being the original vampires. Her current project, The Doll, is her first horror tale, with a touch of mystery. She lives in sunny San Diego, California, with her three dogs, Stuart, Morgan, and Dexter.

Lightning Source UK Ltd.
Milton Keynes UK
UKHW012043060223
416584UK00004B/52